THE MAGICAL FLIGHT
OF DODIE RUE

F.C. SHAW

To Jessica & Jenny

Enjoy the magic of reading!

FC Shaw
2016

The Magical Flight of Dodie Rue

Future House Publishing
Text © 2015 F.C. Shaw
Cover illustration © 2015 Future House Publishing
Cover illustration by Joshua Covey
Developmental editing by Helena Steinacker
Substantive editing by Jenna Parmley
Copy editing by Jenna Parmley and Allie Bowen
Interior design by Emma Hoggan

This book is a work of fiction. Names, characters, places, and
incidents are either the product of the author's imagination or are
used fictitiously. Any resemblance to actual persons, living or dead,
or to actual events or locales is entirely coincidental.

ISBN-10: 0-9966193-3-X
ISBN-13: 978-0-9966193-3-2

To my grandmothers, Eileen and Susan,
For filling my life with magic and for giving me a love for stories
I love you both

Chapter 1

Dodie Rue threw a glance over his shoulder. He slipped down a grungy alley between the village bakery and the butcher shop. The stench of stale bread and rotten meat trimmings was as thick as the desert heat and kept everyone from using this alley as a shortcut to the open-air market. But Dodie had grown accustomed to the smell.

He picked his way over splintered crates and soggy garbage. On tiptoe he neared a clay bowl he'd swiped from his kitchen and propped up with a stick, though now the bowl was turned over on the ground. He heard the scuffling and squeaking of a desperate rat trapped under the bowl. When the rat had scurried into the bowl's shadow to gnaw on a moldy roll, it had tripped the stick and brought the bowl down over itself. It couldn't chew its way out or move the clay bowl—a good trap.

Dodie slid a thin clay roof shingle under the bowl so he could pick up the rat inside. Judging by the weight, he guessed this was a good-sized rat he had trapped. His employer would be pleased. Once a week Dodie set traps for the rats that infested the alley. He could have caught whole tribes of rats easily, but his employer needed only one rat a week.

"Sorry, bud, not your lucky day," murmured Dodie as he tried not to think of the rat's fate.

He carried the rat, trapped between the shingle and the bowl, out of the alley where he turned down the street. He looked around, hoping no one was out this early in the morning yet. His heart sank when he spotted a boy drifting toward him on a magic carpet. Dodie dodged under a shop awning and moved quickly down the street, hoping the other boy wouldn't notice him.

"Hey, Rue!" the boy called. He sidled up to Dodie, his emerald green and gold carpet slowing down. "What are you up to this early?"

"None of your business, Atallah," muttered Dodie as he kept walking down the street.

Atallah Hadi came from the richest family in town and acted like he was superior to everyone else. Though he was only thirteen—a year older than Dodie—Atallah was the best flyer after Dodie's brother. He noticed what Dodie was carrying and smirked. "Oh, your job. Guess every village needs a rat catcher and you're perfect for the task. You're practically a street rat yourself."

"Shut up." Dodie quickened his pace.

Atallah chortled. "If you're hungry my family put

out the garbage last night. You're welcome to it." He zoomed away before Dodie could come up with a retort.

Dodie hated that Atallah, of all people, knew he caught rats for extra income to help make ends meet.

At the next corner an old man spread a mat on the ground. He had unkempt gray hair and a long grizzly beard. His skin was as tan and rough as weather-beaten leather, and he wore a green turban. He sat cross-legged on his mat polishing a long oboe-type instrument, a wicker basket with a lid on the ground next to him.

"'Bout time ya showed up," he barked at Dodie. He jerked his head at the wicker basket. "She's hungry."

"Pretty sure it's a big one today." Dodie held out the clay bowl with the trapped rat.

"Be my guest." The man nodded at the basket again.

Dodie gulped. "Nah, I gotta get back home."

The man's face broke into a grin of missing teeth as he cackled. He took the clay bowl from Dodie. The rat inside squeaked. "Sounds like a lively one." He opened the lid on the basket.

Dodie stepped back a few feet.

The man slid the shingle out from under the rat. It was a large rodent with a bright green, scaly tail. With a terrified squeak, the rat dropped into the basket. Quickly the man put the lid back into place. Dodie caught a small glimpse of the white cobra inside the basket. There was a squeal, a hiss, and then it was all over. The snake charmer gave the trap back to Dodie with another cackle.

"Did ya see that tail? That rat's been mussed with."

Dodie looked at him quizzically.

"Rotten alchemist again," the old charmer muttered. "Until next week then." He tossed a copper coin to Dodie.

Dodie caught it and scampered away. He earned one shek a week catching rats for the village snake charmer's cobra. One shek couldn't purchase anything except for maybe four beans, and that's if the bean merchant was in a good mood. But in a month Dodie could save four to five sheks, and buy two freshly baked pita loaves to share with his family. It was always a good day when he ate bread instead of the usual herb soup his grandfather made, which in reality was just hot water seasoned sparingly with salt and pepper.

When he wasn't catching rats, Dodie worked in his family's shop, Rue's Rug Emporium, which had been selling magic carpets for centuries. Before Dodie was born, the shop had flourished, carrying an ample stock of magic carpets that drew customers from all the surrounding villages.

But then several tragedies struck the Rues in a small amount of time. First, Dodie's grandfather Nadar, who was a racing legend, was crippled in his last magic carpet race, which meant the end of his racing career and the end of prize money to help the family. Second, Dodie's mother died giving birth to him, which left his father Gamal with an empty heart and another child to support. And third, a fire destroyed the shop and burned up nearly all the inventory. Gamal had no choice but to take out a loan to get the business back on its feet. They had been repaying the loan for the last twelve years, always barely making ends meet.

But the Rue's had one spark of hope: the Grand Flyer, a magic carpet race that occurred only every five years. Dodie's older brother Taj was following in their grandfather's footsteps and gearing up for his first race. As the Grand Flyer approached, Rue's Rug Emporium became very busy selling racer rugs.

"I was told Rue's Rug Emporium was the best rug merchant in the region," an elderly woman said, eyeing Dodie behind the counter. "You're sure this is a genuine racer rug?"

"Oh yes, madam. It's been infused with stardust, and like all our rugs, comes with the KVB guarantee." Dodie recited, "It's been Kissed by a genie, Vexed by a sorcerer, and Blessed by the gods. I'm sure you'll be very satisfied with this one, madam."

"Well, it's not for me, now is it?" She opened a silk draw-string purse, dug inside, and counted out ten gold coins. The coins chinked as she handed them to Dodie. "My grandson is entering the Grand Flyer and he needs the very best to ride. He's about your age. You will be racing, too, I suppose? You *are* a Rue, after all."

"Oh, uh, no, it's not my thing," Dodie said, casting his brown eyes down to the money in his palm.

The old woman arched an eyebrow. "What a shame. You *are* Nadar's grandson."

Dodie nodded. "Guess I didn't get my grandfather's racing genes." He laughed politely.

The woman shook her head, muttering as she left the shop, "Tsk, tsk, such a shame."

Dodie cupped the money tightly in his hand and headed to the back of the shop where there was a small room behind a green drape. He entered the purchase in the emporium's ledger, and deposited the coins in a money box that was delivered to their lender every week. Dodie liked that his father trusted him with sales. That helped ease the guilt he felt whenever he heard things like "But you're a *Rue!*" Dodie wished he could fly carpets without breaking into a cold sweat and puking, but it was no use. He was afraid of flying.

"Hey, Dodes!" His sixteen-year-old brother Taj poked his head through the green drape. "C'mon, I gotta get some practice in." He playfully socked his little brother's shoulder. "Got your hour glass on you?"

Dodie followed Taj upstairs. Taj was long and lean and practically all muscle, so he had no trouble bounding up two stairs at a time. They didn't stop on the second or third floors where the Rue boys lived, but continued up to the roof. The flat roof, which doubled as the patio, was lined with empty vegetable planters and cluttered with straw mats, frayed pillows, and tarnished lanterns. Dodie took a minute to catch his breath from the hurried climb as Taj strode over to the edge of the roof where he had left his racer rug rolled up.

"What're you practicing today?" asked Dodie as he plopped down on a mat and crossed his legs.

"Takeoff speed," replied Taj, squatting next to his magic carpet. "That first takeoff when the race starts can make or break you." He held his hand a few inches above his carpet and whispered, "*Sand Surfer.*"

Immediately the magic carpet unrolled its blue and gold tapestry, and hovered a foot off the ground, waiting for its rider. Taj mounted the carpet, sitting on his knees and bending down so his chin grazed the front edge.

"From here to that weather vane," he called to Dodie. "Ready?"

Dodie turned the hour glass over. "Go!"

Taj shot off the roof and straight up into the orange sky. Dodie felt a gust of wind ruffle his shaggy dark hair, and he closed his eyes against the dust raised by Taj's takeoff. He held up an arm to shield his eyes against the late afternoon sun. He saw Taj reach the weather vane mounted on a neighbor's roof, and checked the hour glass. Two and a half seconds. A perfect takeoff.

Dodie looked back up and searched the cloudless sky for Taj. Then he heard hooting and hollering in the alley behind their house. He looked over the edge of the roof and saw his brother standing on his carpet, his knees bent for balance, skimming the tops of the heads of the small crowd that had gathered below. Dodie couldn't help smiling as he pocketed his small hour glass. He spotted Binni, his best friend, in the crowd and bounded downstairs.

Dodie skipped down a narrow side alley to the wider alley where Binni was waiting for him amidst the crowd. Binni was small and skinny with wiry black hair. He always had fresh bruises and cuts breaking out on his face and arms. He claimed they were the price he paid for his alchemy experiments. He lived with his uncle, the town's only alchemist, so had ready access to ingredients and tools.

"Taj is amazing!" exclaimed Binni, giving his buck-toothed grin. "He's the *best* racer in the region. Uncle's sure he's gonna win."

"Show off!" Dodie yelled as his brother whizzed past him.

Taj, still standing on *Sand Surfer*, turned sideways to skim the walls.

"He's threading!" someone screamed ecstatically.

"Oh wow! That's so hard to do," said Binni in awe.

"Atallah's here!" a voice shouted.

Dodie and Binni turned and saw a second rider sailing into the alley.

Atallah rode his emerald green and gold carpet on one bended knee. The crowd noticeably cleared out of his way. He cruised to a stop next to Dodie and Binni. His icy blue eyes landed on Dodie first.

"Where's *your* carpet, Rue? Oh wait, I forgot. You're the one Rue who *won't* fly," Atallah smirked. "Not sure I could live with myself if my grandfather was a racing legend, and I wouldn't set foot on a carpet. What's your deal, you afraid of heights or something?"

Binni jumped in. "He's afraid of flying and pukes whenever—"

"Shut up!" Dodie elbowed Binni in the ribs.

"That's right! Come up with any more potions for him? A waste of time—there's no potion for fear," said Atallah, finally acknowledging Binni. "I don't know if it's worth it, Rue. You don't wanna get the runs again." He snickered.

"You know I'm sorry about that," whispered Binni in Dodie's ear.

"What are you doing here?" Dodie asked Atallah, his eyes narrowing.

"Just checking out the competition." Atallah nodded at Taj who slid a quick landing next to them. "Not bad on the threading," Atallah said in an amicable voice.

Taj gave a sideways grin. "Thanks, how's yours coming along?"

Atallah shrugged in false modesty. "I'd appreciate a few pointers."

"Sure thing. Go for it," Taj said, breathing heavily from his flying antics.

Atallah bent down on both knees and sped off.

"Don't give him pointers!" yelled Dodie, rounding on his brother. "He's a creep!"

"And a bully!" added Binni.

"He's never given me any grief," shrugged Taj.

"That's because he knows you could beat him up,

and beat him in the Grand Flyer," argued Dodie.

They watched Atallah pick up speed down the alley, then suddenly turn sideways and skim the whitewashed walls. At the end of the alley he swooped up, riding for a moment upside down, then turned over and zoomed toward them. He suddenly stopped inches from Dodie's head.

Dodie refused to duck, and tried his hardest not to even blink.

Taj touched knuckles with Atallah and said, "Nice threading!"

"Thanks." Atallah grinned. "I haven't tried threading standing up though."

"You've got plenty of time to practice before the race." Taj hopped on his carpet and took off again.

"So you really can't fly, huh?" Atallah turned to Dodie.

"I can fly," said Dodie. "I just don't like to."

"No, you can't," argued Atallah. "You're *afraid.* You're an embarrassment to the whole village." He leaned in closer. "You're just a poor rat catcher who doesn't have the guts to fly."

Dodie felt his face heat. His heart hammered, and his chest tightened.

"Come on, go for it," taunted Atallah. "Prove us all wrong."

Dodie tried to swallow, but his throat felt as dry as sand.

"Give us a minute." Binni pulled Dodie aside and

said in a low voice, "I have a new potion if you wanna try it right now."

Dodie groaned. "I don't know, Bin."

"If it works Atallah will eat your dust!"

"And if it doesn't?" Dodie looked worried.

Binni shrugged. "That's the chance you take." He opened his palm to reveal a tiny bottle of maroon liquid.

"Hey! Now or never, Rat Scat!" called Atallah, shifting his weight impatiently.

"Fine." Dodie took the tiny bottle, unstopped the cork, and drained the maroon liquid. It tasted extremely sour, as if Binni had squeezed a whole lemon into the potion. He returned to where Atallah waited with his carpet. "Ready!"

Atallah grinned wickedly, held a hand over his rolled up rug, and said, "*Sky Cleaver.*" His carpet opened, and hovered a foot off the ground.

Dodie gingerly placed one knee on the carpet. The carpet stretched tautly and held still. Dodie brought his other knee up and crouched down in a prostrate position. He gripped the two front braided loops, special handles found only on racer rugs. His chest tightened and burned until he realized he had forgotten to breathe. He inhaled deeply.

Dodie stared down the alley behind his house. Lines of colorful laundry stretched across the alley above him. The breeze ruffled his dark hair. Somewhere nearby a donkey brayed. He felt sweat trickle down his cheek even though it was not a hot day. He noticed the crowd had suddenly hushed. Taj had disappeared around the corner.

"Not too late to back out," said Atallah behind him.

Dodie gripped the loops tighter, and tossed a prayer heavenward.

The thought to go was barely in his mind when the magic carpet responded and took off. He shot above the clotheslines and rooftops, then leveled out and zipped around a tower with an onion-shaped top. The carpet grazed a red-tile roof. Dodie looked down and his eyes crossed. He looked ahead at the village skyline and his chest tightened painfully. Below him he heard the crowd cheering, but he couldn't go on. Clearly Binni's potion was not working.

He barely had enough of his senses to coax the carpet down with his thoughts, and he did so too abruptly. The carpet dropped like a stone. His stomach leaped into his throat, then plummeted down again. It felt like his insides were churning, then—

He threw his head over the side and puked, showering the crowd with vomit. Everyone screamed and scattered.

Just land, just land! Dodie pleaded, squeezing his eyes shut.

Finally, it all stopped. His eyelids fluttered open, and he saw the ground a foot below him.

Binni rushed over and grabbed him by the arms, trying to help him up. Dodie shook him off. Atallah laughed. Dodie stumbled to his feet and hastily wiped his chin on the back of his hand. He didn't look Atallah in the eye.

"Don't know what to tell you, Rat Scat," started Atallah as he knelt on his carpet. "Embarrassing—"

"Dodie!" Taj called as he slid to a stop beside them. "What was that all about?"

"Nothing," muttered Dodie.

Atallah shot off, and the crowd dispersed.

"Atallah dared Dodie to prove everyone wrong," Binni piped up.

"Prove everyone wrong about what?" Taj looked confused.

"That the village is embarrassed about Dodie," continued Binni, "because he can't fly."

"What?!" Taj jumped off *Sand Surfer*. "That's not true. How would Atallah know how the whole village feels? You're right—he *is* a creep! Ignore him. Remember what the Seer told you? Someday you'll grow out of your fear of flying."

"That's right!" Binni brightened. "And when that day comes you'll be laughing in Atallah's face."

"In the meantime, want me to beat him up or something?" Taj gave a lopsided grin.

Dodie gave a small smile. "Nah, just make sure you beat him in the Grand Flyer."

Taj threw an arm around his little brother's neck. "No worries there. You saw him, he can't even thread properly!"

Dodie chuckled as they headed back home.

"Hey, and next time you try out flying," said Binni, "do it far away from people. No one wants to get puked on." He waved and crossed the road toward his house.

When Taj and Dodie entered the emporium, they found their father deep in conversation with a tall man in long emerald robes. Gamal Rue looked up at his sons.

"Ah, Taj, over here," he waved the boys over to the counter where he and the tall man stood.

"This is your racer, eh?" the man turned to them.

Dodie knew exactly who this stiff man was and his heart sank. Lord Hadi, Atallah's father, had the same rare icy blue eyes as his son, and held his head up in the same haughty manner. He was dressed in rich emerald robes trimmed with gold thread. His face was narrow and clean shaven with a prominent nose that would have been a feature to make fun of if it was on anyone lesser. But on Hadi it looked regal, and gave him an excuse to look down it at others. He did so at Dodie and Taj.

"My son is excited to race against you, Taj," Hadi said in a smooth voice. "He admires you greatly." He ignored Dodie as he turned back to Gamal. "This will be a good fair bet. Shall we?"

"What bet?" Dodie asked. "What are you talking about?" He looked from his father to Lord Hadi.

"Stay out of this," Gamal said quietly.

"I have the contract all written up." Hadi slapped a sheet of parchment on the counter and whipped out a quill. He scrawled his signature at the bottom of a block of text on the parchment. The signature glowed gold for a moment, then dried into black. He passed the quill to Gamal.

Taj put out a hand to stop his father. "Wait, what are you signing? What is this?"

"Later." Gamal hastily signed his name.

Hadi smiled in satisfaction, rolled up the parchment, and tucked it and the quill into an inner pocket of his robe. He fished out a stone amulet carved into a pair of wings and held it out across the counter. He gripped one wing in his fingers while Gamal gripped the opposite wing.

"I solemnly swear to uphold my end of the bargain," whispered Hadi.

"I swear it, too," answered Gamal.

The amulet glowed blue and snapped apart, leaving both men with a wing. Hadi looked very pleased, while Gamal looked anxious.

"Nice doing business with you, Rue, as always." Hadi swept out of the shop with a swish of his long robes.

"Dad! What deal did you make with him?" Dodie asked.

"Does it have to do with the Grand Flyer?" questioned Taj.

Gamal ran a hand over his haggard face and through his long gray beard. "I made a wager."

"What did you wager?" Dodie felt his pulse

quickening. "We don't have anything!"

"'S why I made the wager." Gamal tucked the wing amulet into his inner pocket and started closing up shop. He wouldn't look at his sons. "Taj wins the Flyer, Hadi forgives our debt to him. Atallah wins the Flyer—"

"He won't!" Taj growled. "I won't let him."

Gamal managed a small smile. "'S why I made the wager."

"But if Atallah does win," interrupted Dodie. "What happens?"

"Hadi owns the emporium," finished Gamal quietly.

"Oh, Dad," moaned Dodie. "We can't lose the shop."

"I won't lose the race," Taj said with steely resolution in his voice.

"What if someone else wins the race?" wondered Dodie.

"Nothing changes," replied Gamal. "We keep paying off our debt to Hadi."

"I'll win," repeated Taj. "Then we won't have our debt, but we'll have the prize money, and I'll have my genie wish, and life will be good!" His optimistic spirit was back, and it lightened the mood.

"Here." Gamal dropped five sheks into Taj's hand. "For the Seer."

"Dad, no." Taj tried to give the coins back. "We can't afford her."

"You gots to get a word from her to get sponsors."

Dodie agreed. "You've gotta have all the help you can get. You gotta beat Atallah."

"Oh I will." Taj pocketed the coins.

Chapter 2

After a usual supper of herb soup that night, the Rues went up to the roof. Lately Taj spent the evenings poring over the race course map and inspecting *Sand Surfer* for loose threads. Gamal left to lock up the village gates, one of the many side jobs he had taken on to pay for Taj's registration in the Grand Flyer. Dodie and his grandfather Nadar stargazed.

Nadar Rue was the racing legend of the county, but now he was a cripple confined to a one-passenger rug. Though Nadar's muscles had deteriorated and old age had set in his bones, he still had the look of a racer. He was long and lean, and he kept his white hair cut short and his face clean-shaven. He never complained about his disability, but there was a hint of sadness in his eyes. He spent his days keeping house and making meals, jobs he had taken on ever since Dodie's mother had died. His carpet, burnt orange and henna colored, bent itself into a chair shape so Nadar could recline comfortably. At night the carpet straightened for him to sleep on.

"Would you like a story tonight?" croaked Nadar, gazing up at the stars.

Dodie nodded. "The one about your last race."

"Again, eh?" Nadar smiled, his face creasing into a thousand and one wrinkles. "Well, you know the Grand Flyer occurs only every five years, and the Grand Renegade is usually the same year after the Grand Flyer. I raced in three Flyers and two Renegades. The third Flyer was my last race. Your grandmother tried to convince me not to race that last one, but I really wanted the prize."

"One wish granted from a genie," recalled Dodie, "and the treasure."

"That's right. The race was typical. There was the usual trek across the dunes, a nice route by the seaside, the occasional band of thieves or run in with a ghoul. But on the last day, a sand storm kicked up. Now, I had flown through my share of sand storms before, but this one was like nothing I'd seen. It was more like a sand hurricane. I thought I could get ahead of it in time to finish the race, but it overtook me."

"But you still won the race," said Dodie.

Nadar nodded. "At great cost. I made it across the finish line and tried to stop, but the wind was too strong. The wind slammed *Phoenix* against the Capital wall. I was riding on my knees, so my knee caps shattered. I fell off *Phoenix* and landed unconscious. When I awoke, the storm had passed and the race officials had finally found me. *Phoenix* had covered me to protect me from the storm. If it wasn't for her, I might have died."

"But carpets don't have a mind of their own," countered Dodie. "Or their own will."

"Ah, but when a carpet and its rider have been together for as long as we were, a special magic forms between them."

"Grandpapa? Do you regret not using your wish to heal your knees? You could have kept on racing."

Nadar gazed up at the black sky glittering with stars. "I chose to make a much more important wish. Someday I'll tell you about it."

⁎

This year's Grand Flyer was scheduled for the first week of spring, so as the last few days of winter waned, the village of Turah was swept up in the preparation and anticipation for the race. Racers campaigned for sponsors, which involved plastering the adobe walls with posters listing their strengths and racing experience, both of which were highly exaggerated (*Racing is in my blood—a blood sample is available upon request*). Gamblers cast their bets, which were officially recorded on a long scroll and locked in Magistrate Oxard's vault. While anyone was allowed to sponsor and bet on any racer from the five competing villages, it was considered near treason to do so for a racer not from one's home village. (One man was refused service at the Wishing

Well because he backed a racer from the next village over.) The race was all everyone talked about, and streets and alleys became hazardous to traverse because the racers were practicing nonstop—or at least were trying to intimidate each other with their threading.

Rue's Rug Emporium was not exempt from it all. Daily the store was bombarded with people purchasing new carpets for the journey to the Capital where the Grand Flyer would finish. Long runner rugs, called Caravaners, were the most popular sale since they carried up to eighteen passengers. Dodie had been spending every day helping in the shop, and every evening helping Taj practice takeoff speed.

Besides the emporium, the Seer was the next most sought after service in the village. Racers, sponsors, and interested parties lined up outside her tent, hoping to hear words of good fortune or prophecies about the Grand Flyer. As a contestant, Taj was expected to visit the Seer, as any word spoken over him would affect his sponsorship. He invited Dodie to go along with him, hoping that perhaps the Seer would have a good word for Dodie in regards to his fear of flying. The two brothers arrived just before closing time. They thought they were the last visitors of the day until Atallah and the village alchemist Raz showed up. They all stood under a tall palm tree shading the Seer's tent.

"Taj, Dodie," Raz greeted with a head nod to each. To Taj he said, "Good luck in the Flyer. Your grandfather must be very proud."

"Thank you, sir. He is," said Taj. "How's the threading, Atallah?"

Atallah grinned at him. "Better. I've been practicing a ton."

Whack! A palm frond whipped through the air and smacked Atallah in the back of the head.

"Crazy tree!" Atallah rubbed his scalp. "You need to do something about it." He scowled at Raz.

A few of the palm trees in town had become victims of Raz's alchemy experiments, and had taken on personalities that ranged from playful to vindictive. Dodie had gotten on the good side of a palm growing by the Wishing Well, and could always count on getting a shower of dates from it. For whatever reason, this palm by the tent had a grudge against Atallah and kept taking swings at him. Atallah dodged away from it, and took a seat on a rough wooden bench outside the tent entrance.

"Listen, Taj," Raz said. "I'll be sponsoring you, no matter what the Seer tells you."

"Thank you, sir!" Taj grinned.

"Of course. You're like family to Binni and me."

A head poked out from the tent. "The Seer awaits," a small withered man whispered to them.

Taj and Dodie ducked through the low doorway and into the tent. The boys stepped over baskets of fresh herbs that made them sneeze, and dodged hanging jars of exotic beetles, lizards, and scorpions. They swept aside layers of sheer fabric until they found the Seer sitting cross-legged on a round pillow. She was shrouded from head to foot in black fabric with a thin, black veil covering her face. Dodie could never tell if she was awake, or asleep, or even if she was looking at him. A large gold pendant engraved with a sun hung around her neck. She was fanning herself, for the tent was very warm and stuffy. The air was thick with incense that made Dodie sleepy. He and Taj sat before her and waited.

The Seer stopped fanning herself and raised a hand over them. She put her head down and rocked gently back and forth. Suddenly she cried out with a loud voice, causing both boys to jump.

"You will triumph over both soul and body and have a change of heart.

At journey's end you will be victorious and find more than you seek."

The Seer stopped rocking and resumed fanning herself. Taj and Dodie waited a few seconds, unsure if she was finished. When she pointed to her money box, they paid her and scrambled to their feet. They stumbled over baskets and ducked under jars and out the tent. They nodded farewell to Raz. Atallah, who was glaring at the palm tree that was still trying to whack him, ignored them as they hurried home.

"So what do you think that prophecy meant?" asked Dodie, hurrying to keep up with Taj's long strides.

"It's gotta be a good prophecy, right? It mentioned I would triumph and be victorious." Taj bounded along with a spring in his step. "Whatever it means it'll get me sponsors."

"Do you think it means you're guaranteed to win?"

Taj stopped in the alley, his tall figure casting a long shadow as the sun set behind them. "I'm thinking it does," he said in an excited whisper. "The Seer's never wrong, is she?"

Dodie's face clouded. "My prophecy hasn't come true yet."

"It will, trust me. You'll fly someday. And don't let anyone get to you—especially Atallah, you hear me? One day you'll make them all eat their words. Plus there's so much more to you." Taj threw an arm around his brother's neck. "I was hoping she'd say some good luck to you." He stopped and turned back toward the Seer's tent.

"Where are you going?" asked Dodie, running to keep up with him.

"Getting you some good luck." Taj stopped outside the tent at a clay pot hanging from the awning.

Painted on the clay pot was *Good Luck Charms 1 shek*.

Taj picked out a small amulet made from clay. It was a burnt red color and had a flame carved on its face.

"Don't spend your last shek on that," said Dodie. "It's just a trinket. It won't bring me luck."

"You don't know that." Taj dropped the shek into the clay pot and handed the charm to Dodie. "Carry it with you for a while and see if your luck changes."

They started for home again.

"Hey, do me a favor and don't tell anyone about my prophecy yet, okay?" said Taj.

✦

Two days before the Grand Flyer the Rues completely sold out of carpets. Dodie excitedly watched his father tally up the sales, and he caught a small smile behind Gamal's beard.

"Is it enough, Dad?" he asked, leaning his elbows on the counter and eyeing the columns of gold coins.

"Hmm?"

"Is it enough to pay off Hadi?"

Gamal looked up at his son, and Dodie's excitement fizzled. His father was looking at him, but his eyes were glassy, which meant his thoughts were far off calculating their plight. Gamal was rarely present. His mind was always elsewhere, usually in the grips of his stress.

"Nah, not enough." Gamal's bushy brows knitted together. "Gots to keep some money to buy more rugs to sell, see?" He scratched a number into his ledger. "'S never enough."

Dodie watched his father, and suddenly realized how old he looked. He had to turn away before he got sad.

That evening they were to attend the Magistrate's Banquet, a special dinner for all the Grand Flyer racers, their families, and sponsors from all five of the competing villages. Everyone dressed in their best clothes and came groomed and smelling of jasmine. The dinner was held in Magistrate Oxard's inner courtyard, a spacious patio laid with turquoise tiles and containing a shallow pool displaying a gorgeous glass mosaic beneath the water. A generous spread of breads, meats, fruits, and wines kept the company full as they mingled around. When the Rues arrived, Taj was immediately whisked away by a large group of sponsors and girls with not-so-secret crushes on him. Dodie spotted the other four racers from Turah: Atallah, Randi the baker's son, Axel the carpenter, and Bae the Magistrate's nephew. There were also plenty of other people Dodie did not recognize, for they were from the other villages.

A small crowd gathered around Nadar, both to pay their homage to the racing legend and to glean tips about winning the Grand Flyer. He generously shared stories with them and signed autographs. Gamal took a few carpet orders from customers. Dodie hung back, unsure of what to do or who to talk to. He avoided Atallah and the other racers, and figured he'd stay away from Taj, too. He didn't want to be that annoying little brother clinging to Taj.

"Is your brother seeing anyone?" a voice behind him asked.

Dodie spun around to face a slender girl wearing too much rouge on her cheeks. "What?"

"Seeing anyone!" she huffed impatiently. "Does he have a girlfriend?"

"Uh, I don't think so."

"Really! Tell him Salarah thinks he's cute and I want to go out with him and I'm dying to ride on a racer rug and I would totally love for him to take me on a ride especially at night under the stars and—"

"Actually he does have a girlfriend," Dodie lied quickly.

"What!" screeched Salarah. "How could he? I'm in love with him and I know—"

"Sorry." Dodie dodged away from her. He was relieved to spot Binni splashing his hand in the pool.

"Hey! You here with your uncle?" he asked Binni.

"Yeah, he almost didn't let me come though."

"How come?" Dodie noticed several fresh bruises running up Binni's arm.

Binni hastily pulled his sleeve down and dried his hand on his lap. "Cuz I got mad at him for sponsoring Atallah."

Dodie's eyes widened. "He told us he's sponsoring Taj!"

"He changed his mind," Binni said. "I'm not happy about it either. I told him Atallah's a bully, but my uncle wouldn't listen to me. Said Atallah's a good bet."

"What about Taj?" Dodie pointed to his older brother who was signing a girl's wrist cuff. "He's sure to win!"

"He said he knew something about Taj that made him go with Atallah."

"What? What does he know?" Dodie felt his insides

27

squirm thinking about Taj's prophecy.

"He didn't tell me," Binni shrugged. "Hey, I finished that new potion. You should try it out tomorrow."

"No offense, Bin, but I'm a little scared of your potions."

Binni looked slightly hurt. "I'm sorry about giving you the runs—"

"And boils! Don't forget that one. Oh, and there was that one potion that turned my pee blue!" Dodie couldn't help laughing at this.

Binni joined him in his laughter. "Sorry! I'm positive this new one won't have any side effects. I tested it on Jinx."

Dodie rolled his eyes. "You forget I'm not a pet tortoise."

The rest of the evening Dodie and Binni talked about the Grand Flyer and their village's five racers. They did their best to avoid Atallah, who followed Taj around and ended up getting two more sponsors by doing so.

The Magistrate made a welcoming speech that was long and boring, and included lots of clichés about unity among the villages and good sportsmanship among the racers, all of which nobody believed in. To prove this a fist fight broke out between Axel the carpenter and a surly racer named Nye from the village Alsta. The guests cleared out of their way, and several sponsors even made quick bets on the fist fight. Magistrate Oxard called for order and repeated a line from his speech about peace and goodwill, but nobody heeded it. Eventually the two racers fought their way out to the street.

The Seer attended the banquet as an honored guest, and while she was not technically on duty, she couldn't help making curt predictions over people. She was still hidden behind her thick veils, which made her look like a ghostly shadow among the living.

"Your cow will get loose tonight," she threw out in passing to a man stuffing bread into his mouth. To another, "She doesn't love you anymore. And you! Yes, you: look under your bed for your missing sandal. Madam, stop lying about your age or a curse will befall you," and so on.

She came up beside Dodie, causing him to jump in alarm. "Rue boy, you must not doubt your prophecy."

Dodie swallowed his bite of lamb. "Yes, madam. But when will—"

"Soon enough. In the meantime, eat up."

Dodie did not have to be told twice to eat more. He went back to the banquet table for several helpings, for he wanted to feel positively stuffed. It had been far too long since he'd had a full belly, and he figured it would be a long time until that happened again. His grandfather's seasoned water wasn't cutting it. He noticed both his father and brother going back for seconds and thirds also.

The Magistrate closed the banquet with a little memorial to his son Petra who had perished in the last Grand Flyer five years ago. Oxard lit a candle, called for a moment of silence, then prayed for the safety and good fortune of all the racers.

It was well past midnight when the Rues finally headed home. Dodie perched on the edge of Nadar's flying carpet. Taj rattled on about his evening as a celebrity, and about the girl Salarah who gave him a kiss.

"You don't look too good," Dodie pointed out.

Taj rubbed his belly. "I think I ate something that didn't agree with me."

"Probably just nerves," Nadar assured him. "Though you do look pale."

When they got home, Taj went right upstairs and collapsed on his bed. He gave a groan as Dodie entered the room.

"You okay?" he asked.

Taj whimpered. "I really wanna throw up. Think I'll feel better if I do."

"I never feel better when I do," mumbled Dodie as he slipped off his sandals.

Taj moaned and rolled over. In a few minutes he was asleep.

Dodie yawned and soon drifted off. What seemed like minutes later, he was awakened by a gagging noise.

"Taj?" he called in the darkness.

More gagging and choking.

Dodie lit the overhanging brass lamp. Taj was shaking, and making gagging noises. Foam bubbled from his open mouth.

"Dad!" Dodie screamed. "Grandpapa! Quick! It's Taj!"

Gamal rushed into the room, followed silently by Nadar on his carpet. Gamal gripped his son to try to steady him.

"Taj! Can you hear me?" Gamal got right in his son's face.

Taj gave one last cough, then fell still, his eyes rolling back in his head.

"Dodie! Get the alchemist, *fast*!"

Dodie bolted downstairs, unlocked the back door, and dodged down the alley. The full moon cast silver beams that lit his way as he skidded around dark corners and ran through the deserted streets. He arrived at the alchemist's shop and banged on the door.

"Raz! Sir! Wake up! Binni!" he yelled, beating the door.

A light turned on upstairs. A few minutes later the door opened. Both Binni and his uncle gaped at him.

"Dodie Rue? What is it?" Raz inquired in a groggy voice.

"Taj," Dodie panted, leaning against the door jam. "Choking . . . gagging . . . he fainted."

"Let me grab my kit." Raz dashed inside.

"He's sick?" asked Binni.

Dodie gulped air. "He ate something bad."

"Let's go." Raz reappeared, carrying a square basket with a handle, and followed the boys back to the Rue house.

Dodie led the way up to the third floor where Taj lay unconscious. Raz knelt beside the boy and examined him. Dodie lingered back, not wanting to get in the way or see Taj lying there like a corpse. Everyone watched Raz, waiting for a diagnosis. With a grave face, he turned to Gamal.

"He's still alive," he confirmed.

"He's sick?" Gamal asked, his calloused hands still gripping his son's arms.

"He's been poisoned."

Chapter 3

"*P*oisoned?"

"By who?"

"By a competitor, perhaps."

"'S there an antidote?"

Raz stood up from kneeling at the bedside. "Give me a few minutes to thoroughly examine him. I have a suspicion which poison was used, but I need to confirm it before I make a diagnosis. If you would all please leave the room." He held out his hand toward the bedroom door.

"Out," Gamal ushered everyone out of the room.

"He'll get better, right?" Dodie asked no one in particular.

"Has to!" Gamal said, tugging on his beard.

"My uncle'll know what to do," Binni said with confidence. "He'll give him a strong antidote. He's the alchemist, after all."

Dodie bit his tongue from arguing that point

with his best friend—the village referred to Raz as the alchemist, but in reality he was more of a physician and pharmacist than a worker of wonders. Everyone knew it was his ambition to someday be a certified alchemist, but he never had enough money to go to the Capital and enroll in formal training. He too had taken a loan from Hadi to purchase his shop and equipment and was paying a steep debt.

Oddly enough, though, a few months earlier, Raz had suddenly started doing remarkable things with potions and elements. Raz gave no explanation for his sudden powers, and no one questioned him since the village benefited from his new knowledge (except for the palm trees, of course). Around that time he demanded the title of Turah's Alchemist, and no one argued.

Raz appeared in the doorway, rubbing his sharp chin that sported a trim black beard.

"Poison?" Gamal rushed to him, his family at his heels.

"It was poison, a very rare and deadly poison called Devil's Kiss," Raz paused, gripping Gamal's shoulder. "It's a wonder anyone was able to get a hold of it. I myself don't carry it in my shop."

"You can prescribe an antidote, yes?" asked Nadar.

Raz's face looked pained. "The only one who knows the antidote to Devil's Kiss is Zalla the Great. And we all know he's—"

"Dead," finished Gamal, rubbing his eyes.

"Who was Zalla the Great?" Dodie asked Binni out

of the side of his mouth.

"The most powerful alchemist of our time," whispered Binni. "The desert swallowed up him and all his work over a year ago."

"What do you mean *swallowed*?"

Binni shook his head, his eyes wide with mystery.

"There is no other antidote," Raz was saying.

Gamal's creases in his forehead deepened. "So . . ."

"The poison will take its fatal effect on Taj in the next seven days. He will die if he does not get the antidote."

Gamal stared.

Nadar choked.

Binni cursed.

And Dodie vomited. He grabbed the closet thing, an empty pitcher, and threw up most of the feast he had eaten earlier at the party . . .

. . . Where someone had poisoned Taj . . .

. . . Where someone had wanted to kill his brother.

"No antidote?" Gamal looked utterly shocked, as if someone had just told him that carpets don't fly.

Raz gripped Gamal's shoulder. "Listen, I will exhaust all my resources and search for the antidote. I will do everything in my power to save your son. But I must be clear, it will take a miracle."

"Then there's still a chance," Nadar spoke up from his floating carpet. "I've witnessed enough miracles in my day to know they can happen."

Raz smiled slightly. "Yes, sir." Turning to his

nephew, he said quietly, "Come, Binni, we have work to do."

Binni gave Dodie a parting wave and left with his uncle.

Without a word, Gamal went back into the boys' room to sit with Taj.

Nadar turned to Dodie. "Pray for a miracle."

Dodie lingered in the doorway, but did not enter the room. After seeing Taj still lying unconscious, he climbed upstairs to the roof. The silver moon was heading west as the early hours of dawn arrived. Dodie lay on a straw mat and gazed up at the stars fading in the brightening sky. He sent a prayer up for Taj.

But his heart wasn't in it.

He knew his grandfather had witnessed many miracles—he had heard of them in his stories. But Nadar had been an extraordinary person; champion of every Grand Flyer and every Grand Renegade he had ever raced in. He had earned the right to believe in miracles.

Dodie had no reason to believe in miracles, for he hadn't witnessed any—not even the small miracle of being cured of his flying fear. He was not a champion of anything.

But right now none of that mattered. Taj was dying. By the end of the week, his brother would be dead. Only a miracle could save him.

Dodie started to think about Taj being gone, but his imagination couldn't stretch that far. Taj had always been there for Dodie and had always made Dodie feel like he mattered, especially when their father didn't seem to even notice Dodie's existence.

Dodie wiped his eyes. He prayed with all his might for a miracle. He wished with all his might for Taj's life to be spared. But again he knew it was no good. He had nothing to wish on, no one to grant his wish—

Dodie sat up.

An idea shot through his brain. There might be one way to have his wish granted, but it seemed impossible.

But the more he thought about it, the more he realized it was the only way to save Taj. And only he could do it.

The problem was he *couldn't* do it.

It was physically impossible.

Unless . . .

Dodie ran downstairs, out of the house, and down the street. He arrived at the alchemist's house once again out of breath. This time he didn't bang on the door; instead he went down a tight alley to the side of the house. He picked up a few pebbles and threw them up at an open window on the second floor.

"Ouch!" Binni popped his head out the window and looked down.

Dodie waved. "I need your help!" he said in a loud whisper.

"Whaddaya need?" asked Binni.

"That new potion you made for me."

Binni's face lit up in the blue darkness. "You want

it now? Sure! It's all ready and I'm sure there aren't any side effects on this one . . ."

Dodie could hear Binni's voice trail off as his friend disappeared into the heart of his house. A minute later Binni joined him outside in the alley. He held up a small glass vial. Even in the gloom, Dodie could see the bright pink hue of the potion. He noticed a new cut on Binni's lip. He appreciated the trouble Binni went through to find him a remedy.

"This is one dose, but I can make more," said Binni as he handed the vial off. "It will last about twelve hours."

Dodie pulled out the cork stopper, gave Binni one last quizzical look, then threw back his head and downed the potion. It was quite bitter. He stared at Binni.

"Should I feel different?" he asked.

"Probably not—except when you're flying a carpet!" Binni said gleefully.

"There's only one way to know." Dodie took off running back home.

"Let me know if it works!" Binni called after him.

Dodie ran back to the emporium, and lit a lamp. In the back room behind the green drape he found his family's Caravaner. He grabbed it under his arm and dragged it to the street. The eastern sky was already lightening. He held his hand over the rolled carpet and whispered, "*Dune Cruiser*."

The Caravaner, a fifteen foot runner rug of gray

and yellow, unrolled. Dodie climbed aboard, tucked his knees under him, and took a deep breath. The carpet started gliding a few feet above the ground. Dodie held on tight and waited for a queasy feeling to set in, but it didn't. He coaxed a little more speed from *Dune Cruiser*. He still felt fine. He decided to take a chance and gain some altitude. *Dune Cruiser* was not a racer rug, so could only rise about twenty feet, but typically that was high enough to get Dodie's stomach churning. This time he didn't feel the slightest flutter. He was growing braver by the minute.

He took a sharp turn, he dropped suddenly, he rose quickly. He felt fine—more than fine, he felt great! He felt free.

Dawn was breaking, the sky turning from deep blue to soft rose. Doors were opening, voices were greeting, and animals were stirring. Dodie drove *Dune Cruiser* back to his home. He hopped off, waited for the runner rug to roll up, then dragged it back inside and leaned it in a back corner of the shop. He bounded upstairs.

He found his father sitting by the window and staring out of it vacantly. His grandfather was boiling water for tea. Dodie felt his insides wiggling, but not from carpet flying.

"I know how we can save Taj," he swallowed. "We can wish for his life."

Nadar looked fondly at him. "If only, my grandson."

"It's the only way!"

"And how do we go about doing that?" Nadar

asked, his gray eyes glimmering with hope.

"I'll race in the Grand Flyer and win the wish." Dodie's insides continued to wiggle. "I'll wish for Taj's life. It's the only way."

Gamal finally looked away from the window and over at his son.

"It's the only way," Nadar croaked, a smile playing on his lips.

Gamal stood up. "You can't fly."

"Binni gave me a special potion for my fear and it works, Dad! I just tested it on *Dune Cruiser*. I've been helping Taj practice for months. I've heard all of Grandpapa's stories. I think I can do this!"

"We've already paid for Taj to race," added Nadar. "What have we got to lose?"

"A whole lot if I don't win," Dodie insisted. "I have to save Taj. Besides, Dad, there's your wager with Hadi, too. I have to save our business."

Gamal stroked his beard and his eyes got that glassy look as his brain started calculating. "You gots one day to get ready." He started to pace and check things off his fingers. "Haircut, racing gear, maps—by the gods!" He smacked his forehead. "A rug! We have any racers left?"

"We sold them all," Dodie felt himself deflating. "And I can't ride Taj's unless he passes ownership to me. He's not even conscious right now!"

Nadar glided over to Dodie. "You need a rug that knows the race, and has enough magic to fly itself when you don't know how." He paused, his eyes sparkling. "You need *Phoenix*."

"Really, Grandpapa?" Dodie smiled.

"Yes!" Gamal thundered out of the room. A minute later he thundered back carrying a rolled up carpet under his arm. He gently set the carpet down, something of reverence in his touch. With a nod at Dodie, he whispered, "Go on."

"Wait, I must pass ownership to you." Nadar glided over to Dodie, grabbed his hand, and pressed it on the rolled up racer rug. "I hereby give *Phoenix* to you, Dodie Rue."

Dodie swallowed. With his hand over the carpet, he whispered, "*Phoenix*."

With lightning speed and a cloud of dust, the magic carpet unrolled, causing everyone to jump back. It was woven with the colors of fire: burning red, vibrant orange, and brilliant blue, creating a flame pattern that was outlined in gold. The carpet stood perfectly still, suspended in the air about a foot off the ground. It stretched flat, as if invisible hands were pulling it taut.

Nadar smiled, his eyes glistening with tears. "She's yours, Dodie."

Dodie rested one knee on the carpet and found it steady. He pulled his other knee on and leaned low. He gripped the gold braided loops at the top, and fixed his eyes on the window. He had barely finished thinking the command to the carpet when *Phoenix* shot out the open window.

Dodie heard his family's whoops of excitement as he climbed higher in the morning sky. The air was cool and fresh as it whipped through his hair and tunic. He had never ridden anything as fast and smooth as *Phoenix*.

He spent the next hour trying everything: turns, loops, takeoffs, landings, riding on his belly, riding up on his knees, riding on his back—he even tried threading. *Phoenix* skimmed walls and rooftops with no effort, and Dodie found his confidence in the carpet mounting. He had never had so much fun in his life. And best of all:

He didn't puke once.

Chapter 4

The rest of the day was spent in a frenzy as they got Dodie ready for the Grand Flyer. Nadar cut Dodie's hair very short, and got to work altering Taj's racing tunic to fit Dodie's much shorter and stockier body. Gamal serviced *Phoenix* with a good cleaning, dusting, and inspection. He also asked Lord Hadi if Dodie could replace Taj in their wager, and Hadi more than happily agreed. Dodie packed Taj's small waist pouch he would wear in the race: small knife, compass, hourglass, and map scrolls. He got Binni to make more potion for him to take. Then Dodie spent hours getting briefed on race tactics by Nadar.

"The Grand Flyer covers five hundred miles in three days," said Nadar as he shuffled through the race maps on his lap. "This year's race starts just outside of town by the Wishing Well, and finishes just outside the south wall of the Capital. It crosses the Fringe, goes through the Dead Lands, and follows along the Siren

Sea. You can expect sand storms, thieves, and ghouls, among other things."

Dodie swallowed.

Nadar continued, "You must reach each check point by sunset of each day, or you will be disqualified. At each check point you will find fresh water, food, and a campsite to sleep. But don't sleep too soundly, for you can't trust anyone and you never know who or what might be lurking in the shadows waiting to rob you . . . or worse."

Dodie gulped.

"You are not allowed to leave the check point until sunrise of the next day or you will be disqualified. There are pit stops along the way where you can stop to get water and food. Fly within sight of other racers, for there is strength in numbers, but don't hesitate passing them to get ahead—use your judgment. Stay high enough to gain some lead, but don't fly too high or you'll get blown off course by the Boundary and be disqualified—trust *Phoenix* and let her set the pace."

Dodie held his head in his hands and meant to grip his hair, but found it was too short now.

"The first racer to reach the Capital before sunset on the third day wins the genie's wish and the treasure." Nadar added, "And the racer *must* be riding the carpet under his ownership."

Dodie nodded, trying to remember everything he was being told. "Any other rules?"

"Well, females aren't allowed to race, but that

doesn't apply to you," Nadar chuckled. "Dodie, the most important thing to know about and the most dangerous aspect of this race is that out on the course there are no rules."

Dodie looked up at his grandfather. "What?"

"There are no rules, no regulations. Anything goes. Use this to your advantage, both to win and to prove your character. Decide what kind of racer you will be."

"What kind were you?"

Nadar shook his head. "You're not me." He held out a small scroll to Dodie.

Dodie took it. The parchment was soft and dusty with age. Carefully he unrolled it to find a faintly drawn map. "Is this a map of the Grand Flyer?"

"Not exactly." Nadar leaned closer and lowered his voice. "This is my own map of secrets I accumulated through the years during my races. Use it to your advantage, and don't let anyone else see it."

Dodie tucked it inside his waist pouch. "Anything else I should know?"

Nadar looked down at him, his wrinkles creasing. "Know who you are. You are Dodie Rue astride *Phoenix*. You are racing for your brother's life."

⭐

Dodie couldn't fall asleep, though it was well past midnight.

What had he gotten himself into? Why did he *ever*

think that he could race in the Grand Flyer and even hope to win? What was he thinking when he told his family he would do it?

He looked over at Taj, now asleep on his side and breathing heavily.

He had only been thinking of saving Taj and his family's business, and it had given him a courage he had never known. He hoped that courage would stay with him when he took off at dawn.

Eventually Dodie awoke to Nadar nudging him. He had gotten only four hours of sleep, but it was better than nothing. He was already dressed in his racing clothes to save time. Nadar had done a good job of altering Taj's white linen tunic, leggings, and head mask, all of which had to be fitted skin-tight. Dodie could still smell his brother's scent on the clothes, and it comforted him. Before heading downstairs, Dodie stopped by Taj's bedside.

"Listen," Dodie whispered softly as he grasped his brother's clammy hand. "*You're* supposed to be racing today, and *you're* supposed to be the next Rue legend— not me. I'm doing this for you. And if I win and make it back alive, I won't owe you another favor *ever*, got that?" He gave Taj's hand one last squeeze, and added, "I told you the Seer is a liar."

His eye spotted the little good luck charm Taj had bought him. He grabbed it from the end table between their cots. When he noticed a tiny hold drilled into the top of the clay charm, he searched for a thread. He plucked a loose string from Taj's tunic and threaded it through the tiny hole. Then he tied the reddish charm around his neck, and slipped it beneath his tunic. It felt cool against his heart.

He bounded downstairs.

Gamal and Nadar were waiting for Dodie in the shop. No words were said. Gamal carried the rolled up *Phoenix* on his shoulder, and led them down the street. As they passed the alchemist's house, Binni joined them.

"Here's your dose for today," said Binni in a hurried whisper. "It's good till sunset."

Dodie threw back his head and gulped down the pink potion. It stung his throat.

As they neared the village gate, they joined a quiet crowd heading for the starting line. Dodie spotted Atallah and his father Lord Hadi walking with their heads held unnaturally high. The baker's son Randi was fidgeting with his waist pouch with trembling hands. Axel showed up sporting a bruised and puffy face from his fight with Nye at the Magistrate's Banquet. Bae was already at the starting line over the hill.

A section for spectators had been roped off behind the starting line, which was marked by a long row of tall torches stuck in the sand. The firelight played an eerie game of shadows and light. Magistrate Oxard, along with the Magistrates from the other four villages, stood under a yurt snacking on grapes and waving to various people as they arrived. As more competitors and spectators joined, the crowd got louder and more excited.

And Dodie's heart thumped faster.

"We better say our farewells here," said Nadar. "The racers will be lining up any minute now." He grabbed Dodie in a smothering bear hug. Dodie inhaled his grandfather's scent, which was the same dusty smell of the carpet shop.

"You can do this," Nadar said firmly, fixing Dodie with his eyes. "Keep Taj in your heart, your eyes ahead, and your grip on *Phoenix*."

Dodie managed a half-hearted smile.

Gamal patted him on the back. "Be safe," was all he said.

A loud gong sounded from the yurt where the Magistrates stood.

"That's the signal to line up," Nadar told him. "Our village is on the left. Go!"

Dodie shouldered *Phoenix*, took one last look at his family, then turned and did not look back. He followed the other racers to the torch-lit starting line. On the left end he found Atallah and the other racers unrolling their carpets. Dodie unrolled *Phoenix*, and when he did, he heard an audible gasp from the crowd. This gasp soon rose to an uproar of excitement as the spectators and competitors recognized Dodie's legendary carpet.

Atallah noticed Dodie, and grimaced first at the flame-colored carpet and then at Dodie. He quickly masked his surprise. "Why are you bothering to race me? A glutton for punishment, huh?"

"I have to race," said Dodie curtly, trying not to squirm from the whole crowd's attention on him.

"Your dad might as well sign over the emporium to my father," Atallah continued with a nasty grin. "Don't worry—you can always be our servants when you're destitute."

Dodie felt his face heating with anger.

Atallah chuckled and addressed the other racers. "I'd stay clear of him—he pukes when he flies."

Randi inched away from Dodie.

The sky was lightening in the east, the stars fading like phantoms. The crowd grew restless with anticipation. More racers continued to line up and unroll their carpets behind the row of torches. Each racer rug had its own unique design and color scheme. Many were jewel-toned with elaborate gold or silver embellishments, but some stood out, especially *Phoenix* and a black and red carpet ridden by Nye.

Dodie's heart was now racing, his arms were tingling, and his stomach was churning. If he hadn't taken Binni's potion, he knew he would already be vomiting. He suddenly had an urge to run away and forget the whole race.

But he couldn't forget Taj. So he turned around, clenched his fists, and set his eyes on the east.

A second gong sounded, and all the racers mounted their carpets. Atallah adjusted his waist pouch so it rested on his lower back. Randi pulled on his head mask. Axel inhaled and exhaled several cleansing breaths. Bae whispered a prayer. Dodie gripped his carpet's loops.

All eyes fixed on the east where Turah lay. The sun was clearly rising, bathing the desert in new sunlight. The crowd was suddenly silent. The yurt flapped in a light breeze, and somewhere from the village a donkey brayed.

Any moment now the sun would peek above the rooftops.

Any moment now the magic carpets would shoot off in the blink of an eye.

Any moment now Dodie would be racing in the Grand Flyer.

He could feel the charm engraved with a flame pressed against his heart, and for the first time he wanted to believe in its good luck.

Dodie's breathing quickened. His palms were sweaty. He was worried about takeoff, about going fast enough, about not falling off. He also wasn't sure when exactly to take off. At the first sight of the sun, or when the whole sun had risen?

His eyes darted at the other racers on either side of him. He would just follow their lead for this first takeoff. Then he would—

Whoa!

A blast of wind and a cloud of sand engulfed him, blinding him. The crowd screamed and cheered. Dodie coughed and blinked his eyes open. He was the only one behind the torches.

Takeoff had happened.

Chapter 5

The crowd roared at him to go.

"Go, *Phoenix*!" he shouted, but the magic carpet had shot up before the words were out of his mouth.

The force of takeoff pulled Dodie's legs out from under him. He gripped his carpet as they gained altitude. He remembered what Nadar had told him about going too high, and the higher he climbed, the gustier the air turned. If he hit the Boundary set over the race course, he would be blown away for miles and be disqualified. He needed to take *Phoenix* down a bit. The magic carpet obeyed his thought and made a smooth dive. Dodie tucked his knees under him and scoured the sky for the other racers. He saw no one ahead of him, and he could no longer hear the crowd behind him. Turah was rapidly disappearing in the past. Ahead and below him lay the Fringe, a vast desert of gentle sand dunes.

The sun continued to rise to his right, which meant he was heading north, so that was good. He remembered from the race course map that this first day he would cover the Fringe and cross the dune range. On the other side of the range was the first checkpoint he had to reach by sunset. He was not off to a good start. He wasn't just in last place, he was virtually in no place.

"What'll I do?" groaned Dodie to himself.

He suddenly remembered the secret map his grandfather had given him. Slowing *Phoenix* down momentarily, he reached behind him into his waist pouch. He found the old scroll of parchment and opened it. His eyes swept over the faint map of the area, and read a few of the nearest locations marked. One caught his eye: *Emergency Stash of Stardust*. Yes! Stardust gave the racer rugs their incredible speed—could even double their speed for a few hours. Perfect!

It was hidden in an oasis palm tree a few miles west of his location. Deviating from the course to stop there would waste even more time, but it was a chance he had to take.

Dodie stuffed the scroll back in his waist pouch, grabbed the braided loops on *Phoenix*, and leaned to the left. Picking up speed again, he flew across more desert until he spotted a clump of green. He circled over a half dozen palm trees, looking below for any sign of people or animals. Seeing nothing but trees, he sailed down into the oasis and landed beside a small pool. He hopped off his carpet, pulled off his head mask, and looked about him.

The oasis was cool, deserted, and quiet. Dodie

checked his grandfather's map once again for directions to the tree which hid the stardust stash. There were no details except a red star drawn next to the words *Emergency Stash of Stardust*. He shouldered his carpet, which had rolled up instantly upon his dismounting, and searched each tree.

The morning sun rose higher in the sky as he became increasingly more frantic. He was just entertaining the idea of returning home and calling it quits when his eyes caught sight of a red mark on the last and furthest tree trunk. Hurrying over to it, he saw that it was the same star as on the secret map. He gave a laugh of relief and set *Phoenix* down. Now where was the stash of stardust?

He walked around the narrow trunk, rapping his knuckles up and down it. The tree did not sound hollow.

Whoosh!

Dodie ducked as a palm frond swept past him, and crouched on his hands and knees. There was no breeze, so Dodie assumed this palm tree had been tampered with by an alchemist just like the ones in Turah. That was odd.

Dodie scuttled on his hands and knees, and searched the base of the trunk. He dug up the sand, thinking perhaps a secret hole could be hidden in the roots. Nothing appeared. Where else did that leave?

Whoosh!

The palm frond swept over his head.

Dodie looked up to the top of the palm. Of course!

His grandfather would not have wasted time landing, he would have flown up to the branches.

"*Phoenix.*" Dodie hopped on his carpet and jetted up. He hovered closer to the top of the palm tree.

The tree seemed fully aware of Dodie now, and fully bent on keeping him from getting any nearer. All its fronds awakened and batted at him. Dodie dodged them as he craned his neck to get a better look between the fronds.

There nestled between the two largest fronds was a small burlap sack with a red star painted on it. Dodie leaned over and made a grab for the sack.

Whack!

He nearly toppled off his carpet as a frond smacked him upside the head.

"Stupid alchemists!" he growled.

He whipped out his dagger from his waist pouch and edged nearer the tree. "Sorry about this."

As one frond swung near him, Dodie chopped it off with his dagger. The tree froze, as if stunned by the attack. Dodie dove for the small burlap sack nestled in the center of the fronds.

His hands tingled as he held the sack. The tree shuddered, so Dodie bolted away. Palm fronds whipped around as Dodie hovered a safe distance from it. Carefully he opened the sack. Silver light glowed inside. Dodie remembered that stardust never decays or loses its potency. He noticed that there wasn't much left, for the sack was only a third full. He hoped it would be enough to infuse his entire carpet.

Dodie had helped do maintenance on many racer rugs in the emporium, so he knew to handle the stardust with caution, for it was very potent. He also knew how to properly apply it. He grabbed the tassel on the back left corner of *Phoenix*, and dipped it into the sack. The tassel, then the corner, then the carpet edges glowed as the rug drank up the stardust. Soon the entire carpet was glowing, its red, orange, and blue colors more vibrant, and its gold edges shining like treasure.

Dodie tossed the empty burlap sack back at the angry palm branches, and pulled his mask back over his head and face. He got into position and gripped the loops, preparing himself for the fastest ride of his life. He could feel *Phoenix* trembling.

Click-click!

Dodie paused, about to take off. He heard the clicking noise somewhere below. He looked down and saw a mound moving beneath the sand toward him. He started to take his carpet down a bit to get a closer look.

Hiss!

He quickly took his carpet up higher as the mound rose, the sand cascading down a large black form. A bright green tail, topped with a stinger, rose straight up. Two enormous curved claws *clicked* up at him. Dodie's mouth dropped open as he watched a giant black scorpion rear up at him.

At first he doubted what he was seeing, for such a creature didn't exist, even in stories. Then he noticed the green tail. Raz must have experimented on a once normal-sized pest. Apparently the results had not been positive.

The scorpion hissed and clicked its pinchers. Dodie gathered his wits and took off.

Zoom!

Dodie felt as if his very skin would be torn off by the wind and friction as *Phoenix* rocketed north. He was flying faster than his thoughts, so he didn't think— he just flew. Below him was a golden blur of sand, and ahead was a blue blur of sky. He couldn't see anything else, and started to worry he would pass the other racers without knowing it, or maybe even the pit stop at this rate. He tried to keep a look out for both.

He flew and flew across the Fringe.

Suddenly he whizzed by something solid. Dodie managed to turn his head and look back, and realized he had just passed a racer. He was catching up. Another racer whizzed by, then another. Dodie reasoned he had better slow down slightly so he could see ahead better and not crash into anyone.

Phoenix slowed enough for him to gain clearer visibility, but still flew fast enough to pass even more racers. Dodie couldn't help grinning—

Then he yelled and threw his arms up to protect his head as he crashed right into a racer directly in his path. The world around him spun as he and the other racer spiraled madly downward through the air. Suddenly they were free of each other—

Ahhh!

—and their carpets.

Dodie had thought flying a magic carpet was thrilling, but nothing compared to free flying in the air with nothing to hold onto. But he wasn't flying—he was falling and plunging to the earth. He flailed his arms and legs as he hurtled toward the sand.

Then he no longer saw the ground. He saw red, orange, and blue flames. He landed on *Phoenix,* and got the wind knocked out of him. For a second he blacked out as he tumbled off the carpet, and landed with a thud on the hot sand a few feet below.

Coughing and gasping for breath, he came to and gingerly sat up. His magic carpet lay rolled up beside him.

"You saved my life," he muttered, resting a hand on the rolled rug.

Nadar was right: there was a special magic in *Phoenix*, a magic that defied standard carpet behavior. Normally a carpet would roll up when its rider was off it, even if that happened in mid-air. But *Phoenix* hadn't, and what's more she had flown on her own accord to catch Dodie.

"All right?" He stared at the carpet, but it did not budge. It stayed tightly rolled as it should.

Well, maybe it had just been luck that *Phoenix* had been in the right position at the right moment to catch Dodie.

Dodie heard a muffled moan nearby, and

remembered the other racer he had collided with. The racer was sitting up and rubbing his shoulder, his rug nowhere in sight.

"I'm sorry!" called Dodie as he slowly stood up. "I didn't see you. You okay?" He headed toward the racer, his feet sinking in the hot sand with each step.

The racer stood and rushed at Dodie, his fists swinging. Dodie held up his arms in defense.

"I know you're mad!" Dodie braced himself for the hit.

When the punches came, they weren't that hard. Dodie swung back, connecting with the racer's shoulder, causing the racer to stumble back. With dark eyes flashing behind his mask, he charged at Dodie again and this time knocked him to the ground. The two tumbled over each other in the soft sand. Dodie felt the boy's arms as they wrestled, and they did not feel very muscular.

"Hold on!" Dodie tried to get up, but the racer gripped him around the neck.

Dodie reached up, feeling for the boy's head, and grabbed the boy's head mask.

The racer shrieked as Dodie ripped it off.

Dodie gasped at the unmasked racer. "You're a . . . a girl!"

The racer stood panting, her cheeks flushed and an angry scowl across her face. She had thick black hair cut short just below her ears.

"What're you doing—you're racing?" Dodie

stammered.

The girl rolled her large brown eyes. "Not anymore!"

"So sorry for crashing into you! Don't worry, your racer rug's gotta be around here somewhere." Dodie started searching the dunes.

"Doesn't matter anymore! You know I'm a girl."

Dodie stopped to look at her. "So?"

"So I'll be thrown outta the Grand Flyer once they find out. Girls aren't allowed to race!"

Dodie's eyes widened. "How did you enter the Flyer?"

"I registered under another name," she huffed in annoyance. "I went to a lot of trouble to be here, and now it's over!" Her eyes blazed with a fierce fire that Dodie found both intimidating and fascinating.

Dodie stared at her a minute. "Well, maybe I won't say anything right away."

Her expression softened. "Why not?"

"It's none of my business," he shrugged. "Let's find your carpet."

"It's no use," she said, her voice catching. "We're way behind now."

Dodie spotted her racer rug rolled up on the other side of a gentle slope. He trudged through the sand and picked it up.

"I'm Dodie from Turah," he said as he passed off her rug.

She eyed him a moment before saying, "I'm Zinnia from Alsta."

"Nice to meet you, and good luck." Dodie got back on *Phoenix*.

Zinnia muttered, "*Amethyst*," and her racer rug unrolled, its graceful fuchsia, cerulean, and silver swirls gleaming.

Dodie was about to take off, but he didn't feel right about leaving her behind, especially since it was his fault she would now be in last place. "I have an idea of how we can both catch up."

Zinnia pulled her head mask back on. "You shouldn't help me. I'm a competitor."

"It's my fault you're behind now. The least I can do is help you catch up, then you're on your own," Dodie said matter-of-factly.

"What's your idea?' asked Zinnia as she knelt on her carpet.

"Hold onto the back of my carpet. I mean, really hold on."

Zinnia grabbed one of *Phoenix's* back tassels with one hand, and gripped *Amethyst's* braided loop with the other.

They took off instantly. Zinnia squealed in surprise, which made Dodie laugh. They streaked through the sky, and within minutes they passed two racers, then three more. An hour later they spotted a bright red yurt pitched in the sand below. Other racers were already parked there, and more were arriving. Dodie skidded to a stop.

Zinnia stepped off her carpet. "Normally I'd say I

owe you one, but this is a competition. I mean to win."

Dodie could see that fire in her eyes again. "Me too."

She leaned in closer to him. "And just because I'm a girl don't think I can't beat the best of you."

Dodie felt slightly annoyed that she was being brisk with him after he just helped her catch up. He wondered if he should turn her in, but he did believe it was none of his business. He had no right to judge why she was there or if she deserved to race. After all, by all rights, he did not deserve to be racing against the top flyers in the region for the most coveted prize. He couldn't call himself a racer by any means. Besides, if she was brave enough to disguise herself and enter a race against boys, she deserved a chance to do just that.

Without warning, Dodie found himself admiring her.

Chapter 6

About half of the twenty-five racers had stopped to refuel, while the others sailed on by with catcalls. Everyone from Turah stopped.

The red yurt housed a stone well amply supplied with fresh cool water from an underground spring. There were also baskets of bread and bananas for the racers. The yurt was spacious enough to offer everyone a shaded break from the sun. Zinnia kept her facemask on, and adopted more boyish mannerisms, like downing her water in one gulp, ripping open her banana with her teeth, and sitting with a stooped posture. Dodie was sure that if he hadn't unmasked her, he would have had no idea she was a girl.

Dodie rolled up *Phoenix* and carried her under his arm. Inside the yurt he scarfed down a banana and a slice of pita bread while he waited in line for another drink at the well. This snack was better than anything he'd been eating at home, and he snuck a second helping.

"Don't eat too fast or you might throw up, Rat

Scat," Atallah called over to Dodie.

Several racers snickered.

"Sorry about Taj," continued Atallah without the faintest hint of sympathy in his voice. "Yeah, what happened?" Randi, the baker's son, asked. "How come you're racing?"

"He's sick," said Dodie.

"He was poisoned," elaborated Atallah as he finished off his banana. "Who did it?"

"Not sure," Dodie said crisply.

"So you're taking Taj's place?" Axel asked, suddenly interested in the conversation.

"Like you even have a chance," finished Atallah with a shake of his head.

"*We* have a chance now!" exclaimed Bae with a grin. "Taj was the best. With him outta the running this competition just blew wide open!"

Dodie felt his throat tightening as he pictured Taj lying on his death bed. He couldn't think of anything biting to reply with. Taj always knew what to say to people, especially when they picked on Dodie, but out here Dodie was on his own. He caught Zinnia looking at him, but quickly turned to the well before she could see his eyes watering. He drank several cups of water, and felt refreshed. He gobbled down another piece of pita bread and was about to leave the yurt when he heard Atallah shout to Zinnia, "Do I know you? Where're you from?"

Dodie spun back around in the doorway.

"None of your business," Zinnia said in a harsh voice. She marched out of the yurt, bumping Dodie's shoulder as she did.

Atallah watched her go, his eyes flashing.

Dodie went outside and unrolled *Phoenix.* Next to him Zinnia hopped on *Amethyst.* Atallah stormed out of the yurt.

"Hey!" he yelled at Zinnia, who did not turn to look at him. As Zinnia flew off he shouted, "Coward!"

"Shut up!" Dodie snapped as he knelt on his carpet.

"What did you say?" Atallah unrolled *Sky Cleaver* and mounted it.

"I told you to *shut up!*" Dodie couldn't believe the anger he was feeling. "And while you're at it, eat my dust!"

Phoenix shot off, but to his dismay it wasn't at stardust speed, rather at mere racer rug speed. The stardust had run its course. He knew it couldn't last forever, but he'd hoped it would have lasted long enough for him to leave Atallah gasping in his wake. Instead Atallah was right behind him.

Dodie kept his eyes ahead and his grip firm on the braided loops.

A shadow cast over him. Then Atallah's green and gold carpet grazed his face. Atallah was threading on him.

Dodie swerved away as Atallah zoomed ahead, laughing.

For several hours, Dodie kept a good air speed,

staying ahead of several racers, but still within eyesight of the larger group. They crossed mile after mile of red sand and soft rippled dunes. There seemed to be no end to the Fringe. As the afternoon wore on, the temperature climbed. Dodie tried not to fly too low, for the sand gave off a dry heat. He also felt the sun's rays burning through his skin-tight white linen tunic and leggings. He thought about the red yurt with its shade and well of cool water more and more as the heat continued to rise. His legs were cramping up, and his back was aching. He also had to pee. He noticed the racer Nye, riding a black and red carpet, scoot his legs out from under his body and stretch. Dodie copied him, and felt immediate relief in his legs. He stayed flying like this, stretched out on his belly, for another hour, and caught himself dozing off once or twice. Nearby a thudding sound snapped him to his senses. He turned quickly to look behind him, and saw a racer rolling down a dune.

Atallah, flying nearby, laughed. "Idiot! Must've fallen asleep!"

Dodie blinked his eyes and slapped his face to make sure he stayed wide awake now.

Across the Fringe, he spied a snaking figure a few miles ahead. As he flew closer, he saw a long single line of camels slowly trekking across the dunes. There must have been over fifty camels, all packed with bundles and riders sheathed in layers of fabric. Several camels dragged large metal boxes that made smooth tracks in the sand.

The racers tensed, tightening their grips and tucking their legs under them, and a few rose higher in the air. Dodie wondered what they had to be worried about, so he pulled *Phoenix* back a little, letting the front racers pass over the merchant caravan.

As soon as the flying carpets neared the caravan, the merchants jumped off their camels and hurried to the metal boxes. They threw open the tops and a swarm of flying creatures of different colors burst out of the boxes and took to the sky. They screeched and headed straight for the racers, their leathery wings stirring up the air.

Dodie couldn't tell if they were birds or bats or—

"Dragons!" he yelled, partly in awe and partly in terror as jets of fire shot from the flock.

The dragons were small, about the size of hawks, and varied in color from blood-red to poison-green. Their scales shimmered in the sunlight as they zipped around at incredible speeds. Four dragons attacked the front racer on an orange and blue carpet by spitting fire at him. The racer's tunic ignited, and with a scream, he fell off his carpet. He somersaulted downward through the air, and crashed on the sand. A golden dragon and a royal blue dragon caught his magic carpet midair in their front claws and flew off with it. When they dropped the carpet near their caravan, it rolled itself up and landed with a plop. The merchants on the ground carried off the racer rug.

The racer who had fallen was rolling around in the sand trying to extinguish the flames eating up his clothing. Just as he managed to, the merchants fell upon him and beat him furiously, leaving him unconscious in the sand.

Dodie gulped as he watched the dragons head toward him and the other racers. Atallah expertly dodged shooting flames. Out of the corner of his eye, Dodie saw Zinnia whiz by him.

"No! Wait!" he shouted to her.

She didn't look back. A purple dragon screeched and spit fire straight at her, but she pulled up *Amethyst* and swerved to the right, missing the flames.

Dodie was worried, for he had no skills when it came to advanced flying. He hoped *Phoenix* would make up for it. He heard a thud and a scream on his right. Another racer fell burning through the sky and landed in the sand below him. His carpet was snatched up by the merchants before he could even get to his feet.

"You gotta help me out," Dodie mumbled to *Phoenix.*

He scanned the swarm of dragons ahead, trying to pick out which ones were aiming at him. Dodie remembered there was strength in numbers, so he dove over to Atallah, Zinnia, and Randi who were fending off flames, and rode their drag. The same purple dragon was still gunning for Zinnia, pelting fire at the underside of her carpet. While the fire did not burn the carpet, its force threw her off balance. Dodie, riding behind her, closed the gap between their carpets, and shot out a hand to steady her. She regained her position.

A screech sounded near Dodie's head. He ducked lower as flames sprayed over his head. He kept close to the group. Suddenly *Phoenix* rolled up her left side over Dodie, and he felt a hot blast hit her underside. The flames extinguished with a sputter.

"Thanks!" he shouted to his carpet.

"Ahhhhh!" screamed another racer nearby as he fell headfirst to the earth. A team of dragons dove after him and snatched up his carpet.

Dodie could see the end of the caravan ahead.

Sizzle!

Fire struck Dodie's left shoulder. He shrieked as the flames devoured his sleeve and licked his skin. He rolled against his carpet and was relieved when the fire extinguished. He heard an angry screech and saw two red dragons swoop up and grab hold of his carpet in their claws. They yanked.

Dodie's left hand lost its grip on the braided loop, and he slid sideways, his feet dangling off the edge. The imbalance caused *Phoenix* to lurch.

"Steady!" he hollered at her, but he knew she wouldn't be able to right herself with two dragons clutching her.

The dragons yanked *Phoenix* in an attempt to shake Dodie off. He held on.

He felt them lose altitude. As he peered below, he could already see the gang of bandits running beneath him, ready to catch his rug and kill him.

The ground was rushing up too quickly. He could now make out the eyes and noses and teeth on the merchants.

The red dragons shook his carpet. Dodie could see the dragons' bellies under *Phoenix*. He brought up his legs and kicked their bellies as hard as he could. Both dragons roared in surprise and lost their grips on *Phoenix*.

Dodie reached up, grabbed the other loop, and flung himself on top of his carpet. In a blink, *Phoenix* blasted straight up into the sky. Dodie hung on for dear life. He could hear the dragons screeching and blasting fire behind him. After a moment he no longer heard them, and he noticed how high he had climbed, for he saw mountains of clouds instead of sand. He did a nosedive.

Far below racers were dodging flames and heading for the dune range. The swarm of colorful dragons was thinning as they returned to their metal boxes. The merchants must have decided they had enough carpets and didn't want to lose their dragons in the dune range. Soon the sky was clear and the caravan continued on its journey west.

Dodie felt empowered. He had just fought off fire-breathing dragons!

The nearer he flew to the dune range, the larger the dunes were. They were the size of mountains, and stretched as far as the eye could see from east to west. The check point lay on the other side of the range. At the foot of the sandy mountains, everyone halted.

Dodie couldn't remember what Taj had said about the dune range. He remembered Taj studying the course map, and preparing himself for all the hazards along the way, but Dodie hadn't really paid attention. Why would he? He never imagined he'd be in the Grand Flyer atop a racer rug, staring up at these towering sand dunes.

Atallah whipped off his head mask, shook out sand, and put it back on. Axel pulled out a tangle of ropes and proceeded to tie his legs and arms to his carpet's tassels. Bae sent a prayer up to heaven. Zinnia took out a small brass compass and tied it to her rug's braided loops.

Dodie wasn't sure what to do, so he spread open his grandfather's secret map, hoping there was something helpful concerning the dune range. Next to the small drawing of the sandy mountains was scrawled *Ride the tail for smooth passage*. He stuffed the map back into his waist pouch, and joined the group as they took off again for the dunes.

The wind grew steadily stronger as they entered the range. By the time Dodie had reached the range's summit, he was having quite a time staying on his carpet, for the wind was so gusty. He held on tightly as the gusts jostled him from side to side, and sometimes even from behind. The going was slow.

Suddenly a shadow passed directly overhead, and Dodie looked up. Gliding smoothly above him was a creature Dodie had heard rumors about but had never dreamed he'd see. The creature had an impressive wingspan of black feathers, and had sharp front talons. Its head, with acute amber eyes and a hooked beak, resembled an eagle's. The rest of its body was sleek and muscular, resembling a bronze furred lion. Its back legs were tucked up and a long tail trailed behind.

A gryphon.

The gryphon glided effortlessly above him, and soon was passing over Dodie with not so much as a ruffled feather.

Nadar's clue suddenly made sense, and Dodie knew it was telling him to follow the gryphon. But Dodie remembered the legends about gryphons being fierce warriors that guarded treasures. They were called kings of the animals. Those razor talons, sharp beak, and powerful hind legs defended that title. No wonder the dragons had turned away from the dune range, for they were mortal enemies to gryphons. Dodie was not in a hurry to trail such a beast.

The wind grew stronger, and while Dodie struggled to stay atop his carpet and plow through, he noticed the gryphon flew with ease. Dodie climbed up, the wind battering him from all angles.

Then the wind was gone. The gryphon was sailing on a smooth jet stream above the tumultuous wind. Dodie followed behind at a safe distance. He cast his eyes below to watch his competitors battling the gale. They were getting further behind.

He continued to follow the gryphon through the

dune range, and was starting to get drowsy again when the gryphon veered west. Dodie sat up straighter. The checkpoint was north on the other side of the dunes, so he kept his course straight while the gryphon turned left.

"Ahhh!" Dodie wailed as a forceful gust of wind slammed him.

Quickly he veered left and followed the gryphon to the west. He was back on the peaceful air current. This gryphon clearly knew the smoother path, so Dodie stayed with him. Occasionally the gryphon would zigzag east and west, or glide a few feet higher or lower, and Dodie kept right with him.

At one point the gryphon opened his hawk beak and screeched. Dodie tensed and readied himself to make a dive should the gryphon notice him and attack, but the gryphon continued on without glancing behind him.

The red sun hung low on the western horizon, and soon slipped behind the dunes. Dodie started to worry he wouldn't make it to the checkpoint before sunset. He had lost sight of his competitors an hour ago, and hoped they were still behind him. Maybe if he was the first one to reach the checkpoint, even if it was after sunset, he would be spared disqualification. He doubted it though, since checkpoint rules were really the only strict rules of the Grand Flyer.

The air felt cooler, and the sky had turned from blue to deep purple.

And then Dodie saw it: the checkpoint. On a sandy plain beyond the dunes, campfires and tents made a merry welcome. Another mile and he and the gryphon had cleared the dune range. The gryphon soared east, while Dodie zoomed for the checkpoint. As he glanced west, the sun kissed the horizon.

Dodie's stomach churned. He didn't know why he was so nervous, he was almost there. He would make it.

His middle gave a sickly lurch and started convulsing. And then it dawned on him: Binni's potion had run its course.

"Al . . . most . . . there . . ." he said through gritted teeth, thinking that would keep the vomit down.

His head got dizzy. His hands turned clammy. His stomach was erupting. His fear was back.

With one last burst of speed, he slid into the checkpoint and tore off his head mask. He didn't hear the applause from the race officials.

He was busy throwing up.

Chapter 7

Once Dodie was able to stand upright without feeling dizzy, he found himself encircled by a group of race officials, their faces beaming at him in the fading daylight. They wore long robes of loud colors like orange, turquoise, scarlet, yellow, and lime green. There were five in all, one representing each competing village. The official from Dodie's village, who he recognized as Oban one of the Magistrate's counselors, came forward and shook both his hands at once. He was dressed in turquoise robes.

"Well done!" Oban smiled as he kept shaking Dodie's hands. "You are the first racer to reach the checkpoint tonight!"

"Name please?" an official in orange asked. He poised a quill above parchment.

"Rue," answered Dodie, feeling his arms were about to fall off from the enthusiastic hand shaking.

"Of course! You're a Rue—no wonder you placed first today. Great start to the race, Taj!"

Dodie's face fell. "Oh, I'm not Taj."

The two officials peered closer at him.

"By the gods, you're not!" said Oban.

"I'm confused, who are *you?*" asked the orange official.

"I'm Dodie. Taj is my older brother. He's . . ." Dodie swallowed down a lump in his throat he had not expected. ". . . very ill. I'm racing for him."

The group of officials whispered amongst themselves. For a moment Dodie felt nervous they might disqualify him, throwing some rule at him about riding in another racer's stead.

Oban turned to him. "We are very sorry about your brother and wish him health."

"Good luck in the remainder of the race, young Rue," the official in orange winked at him.

At that moment, two racers dove into the checkpoint, followed closely by a few others. Dodie tried to see who they were, but the gray light and campfire shadows made it hard to distinguish people. He did spot Atallah whipping off his head mask.

"What place? First?" he panted at the officials.

"Second place, well done!"

"*Second?* Who was first?" he demanded, his hands on his hips.

"Dodie Rue!"

Atallah gaped at Dodie. "What! I didn't see you anywhere. How did you get here *first?*"

Dodie shrugged, enjoying the moment. "I know a

few tricks."

Atallah got in his face and narrowed his eyes. "I know a few tricks, too. You better watch your back." He stalked away.

"You're a target now," a voice behind Dodie said.

Dodie turned and smiled at Zinnia. "Guess people'll start taking me seriously in this race."

"So should you." Zinnia walked off to a campfire.

The sun had disappeared and early stars were waking. Two late racers glided into the checkpoint, and were disqualified. Dodie felt a huge lift in his spirits having not only qualified for another day, but having earned first place. He started to believe that he might even win this race.

But he still had two more days, and the stress sent wiggles through his gut.

"Rue!" Oban beckoned to him. "Listen, arriving first place at the checkpoint warrants you a special advantage."

Dodie straightened up. "Really? I didn't know that! What is it?"

"You are allowed to take off earlier tomorrow. I will wake you just before sunrise."

Dodie smiled.

"Best of luck to you. Get some rest tonight." Oban joined his comrades in a large yurt.

The officials' yurt, stationed next to a stone well, stood in the center of the checkpoint with small campfires encircling it. Racers sat in twos and threes, mostly with their village kinsmen, around campfires, swapping stories of the day. All of them, except for Zinnia, had their head masks off. Some washed their faces and necks with water from the well, while others kicked off their sandals. Everyone kept his racer rug rolled up right next to him. Soon the officials passed out cups of goat's milk and baskets of bread, roasted lamb, and dates to the racers.

Now that Dodie's stomach had emptied and settled down, he was famished. At first he wasn't sure where to sit, or who to sit with. He found the other racers from Turah at one campfire and joined them. Atallah was already telling a much embellished story of his day to the others. He smirked as Dodie plopped down in the sand, and opened his mouth to say something.

"Shut it, Atallah," Dodie snapped. "Nothing you say to me is gonna make me quit. I'm here, I'm racing, and I came in first place tonight, so just shut it."

The other racers stifled chuckles. Atallah glared at everyone, then shot to his feet and stomped off to the well.

Randi clapped. "Thank you, Rue!"

"I can't stand him," muttered Axel.

"You can't stand a lot of people," chuckled Bae.

"True, but I *really* can't stand Atallah," Axel glowered as he polished off his goat's milk. "And that Nye from Alsta."

Dodie listened to Axel recount his fight with Nye at the Magistrate's Banquet. It had started with Nye saying something inappropriate about the girl Salarah. When Bae teased Axel about liking her, he didn't deny it. Dodie thought it best not to mention Salarah's impetuous kiss for Taj.

When they finished their dinner, they stretched out on the sand and lay their heads on their rolled up racer rugs. Soon they were peppering Dodie with questions about Taj and *Phoenix* and why Dodie could suddenly fly. He did not tell them about Binni's potion.

Axel got up to get a drink from the well, and Dodie joined him. They both shouldered their carpets and headed over to the well where two shadowy figures loitered. As they neared them, they recognized Atallah's boisterous voice. Nye was with him.

"I was just talking about you, Rat Scat," said Atallah as Dodie and Axel walked up. "Telling Nye how you're scared of flying."

Nye crossed his arms and pierced Dodie with a glare, his thick black eyebrows knitted together.

Atallah took a step closer to Dodie. "How come you're able to fly now? What's your secret?"

Dodie drew himself up a bit. "Yeah, I've got a secret," he said. "I'm gonna beat you. Wait, guess it's not a secret anymore."

Axel snickered, Atallah scowled, and Nye kept glaring.

Atallah got right in Dodie's face. "Be careful, Rue, and watch your tail tomorrow. There is *no way* I'm getting beat by some air-sick rat catcher on his grandfather's rug. No way!" He stormed off to his campfire.

Axel whistled and dipped a cup into the well. "I think you just woke a monster, Rue."

"I know," groaned Dodie. "How'd the race go for you today?"

Axel set his cup of water on the edge of the well, and started recounting his narrow miss with the dragons and his gusty journey through the dune range. His back was turned to Nye, so he didn't see Nye's quick movement, but Dodie did. Problem was he wasn't sure what he saw. Nye's hand moved forward, and the shimmer of glass in the moonlight caught Dodie's eye for a second. Then Nye left them.

"I know we're competitors and all," Axel was saying, "but I want you to know I respect what you're doing."

"Thanks," said Dodie, taking a swig of water.

"Doesn't mean I can stand you though," Axel grinned and downed his cup of water.

"Right," Dodie grinned back.

He left Axel at the well and traipsed back among the racers, most of whom were asleep. He was about to rejoin his kinsmen at their campfire when he noticed Zinnia sitting alone at a campfire farthest away from everyone. He walked over to her.

"Mind if I sit with you?" he asked.

Zinnia shook her head, gazing into the fire. She still wore her mask.

Dodie plopped down next to her and set his rolled

up *Phoenix* beside him. He watched the flickering flames light up her masked face with an orange glow. Now that night had set in, the desert had cooled considerably, and the fire's heat felt soothing and helped him relax.

The black sky looked bigger than it did back at home, and the stars shined brighter. Dodie thought about his family, wondering if there had been any change in Taj. He thought about his grandfather, and was already looking forward to telling him how he had used his secret map twice on the first day. As he lay there star gazing, his body suddenly felt exhausted and all he wanted to do was roll over and sleep for a long time. But Nadar had warned him about sleeping too soundly, and he wondered how to go about not doing that.

Oban approached them, and both Dodie and Zinnia scrambled up to show respect.

"Rue!" he chimed with enthusiasm. "I need to send a brief report back to Turah, and would like to ask you a few questions. Your family will want to know how you are. It's good publicity. Follow me."

Dodie left Zinnia to follow Oban into the officials' yurt. There was another stone well, slightly smaller than the one outside. A faint wisp of golden dust wafted up from its opening, and Dodie knew it was a Wishing Well. He stepped up to it with Oban.

"Be sure to speak up so our correspondent at Turah's Wishing Well can hear you," Oban instructed. He cleared his throat and barked into the well, "Come in, come in, this is Oban. Do you hear me, Jamar?"

There was a pause, then a hollow voice echoed up from inside the well. *"I hear you loud and clear. Begin your interview."*

Oban turned to Dodie. "How was your first day?"

"It was alright," Dodie said at first, then thought more about his day. "Well, it didn't start out too good. I didn't take off fast enough and was in last place."

"Really! How did you manage to catch up?"

Dodie hesitated, remembering his grandfather's order to keep the secret map hush-hush. "I had a little stash of stardust and used it for extra speed."

"What was that last part?" the voice inquired from inside the well.

"Repeat that last part again for Jamar," muttered Oban.

Dodie leaned his head over the well and repeated the bit about using stardust to catch up.

"That's brilliant!" Oban praised. "Tell me more about your brother Taj and the reason you're racing in his stead."

With some effort to keep his emotions at bay, Dodie told him all he knew, except for the part that his brother would die if Dodie didn't win. He had to repeat a few words into the well. When he was finished with the interview, Dodie returned to Zinnia and sat back down by the campfire.

"I'm sorry about your brother, really—I couldn't help eavesdropping," Zinnia told him quietly. "It's horrible that he was poisoned."

"That's not the worst of it," muttered Dodie. "Taj is gonna die."

Zinnia inhaled sharply. "There's no antidote?"

"No. He'll die by the end of this week . . . unless . . ."

"Unless you win and wish for his life," finished Zinnia.

"Yeah. I never would've taken his place and raced for anything less. This isn't my thing."

"Yeah, I kinda got that." Zinnia glanced at him. "Do you know who poisoned Taj?"

"No, but I hope whoever did will hang for it. Pretty sure it was someone at the Magistrate's Banquet. Were you there?"

"No, I couldn't wear a mask to the party!" Zinnia exclaimed, sounding like a girl again. "Do you think another racer poisoned Taj?"

"Or a sponsor. Taj was the favorite to win. But who'd go to the extreme of poisoning him?" Dodie muttered more to himself as he started going through the guests at the banquet. "And not just to keep him from racing, but to actually kill him? Why wasn't it enough to just make him sick and unable to compete?" He suddenly gasped.

"What's wrong?" Zinnia started.

Dodie looked at her, weighing whether to tell her or not. "The Seer made a prophecy over Taj. It was a powerful one. It would be a good motive for taking Taj outta the race."

"Did anyone else overhear it?" Zinnia asked, very interested.

"Raz the alchemist and Atallah Hadi might have. They were waiting right outside her tent," replied Dodie, his voice dropping in suspicion. "If Taj were to die, there's no way that prophecy could come true now or even later through the years in future Grand Flyers."

"Good point." Zinnia lay down on her rug. "Which poison was used?"

"Taj was poisoned by Devil's Kiss. Raz said it's extremely rare and he doesn't sell any."

"Better keep your eyes and ears open."

"You okay to be camp buddies tonight?" Dodie asked Zinnia.

"Sure," she replied, sounding sleepy. "Can I trust you not to steal my racer rug or stab me in my sleep?" She said this last part with humor in her voice.

"You can trust me," Dodie said sincerely. "Let's take shifts on guard duty. I've got my hour glass. You sleep first. I'll wake you in two hours."

Zinnia rolled over onto her side facing away from Dodie.

He soon heard her breathing deeply. He knew Zinnia was his competition, and he knew he had to beat her. But in the meantime, he was liking her company, and strongly felt he could trust her. He especially appreciated her sympathy about Taj.

As the hours crept by, Dodie found his eyelids

growing very heavy, and decided to stretch his legs and get his blood circulating again. He paced around a little, keeping Zinnia in his sights. As he paced closer to a nearby campfire, he heard someone coughing violently. Axel was writhing on the ground and gagging. Dodie rushed over to him.

"Axel! You okay?" Dodie patted him on the back.

"I . . . can't . . ." *Cough-cough!* ". . . breathe . . . get . . ." *Cough-cough!* ". . . help!" Blood was oozing down his chin.

Randi and Bae woke up, and huddled around Axel.

"Hang on!" Dodie dashed for the officials' yurt. "Help! I need help!"

Several officials darted out.

"It's Axel! He can't breathe!" Dodie scrambled back to the campsite, the officials right behind him.

Axel was on his hands and knees, still coughing hoarsely. Randi smacked his back while Bae ran off to fetch water. Oban grabbed Axel's face in his hands and studied him.

"Bitter-root poison!" he announced. "I have an antidote in my case!"

Oban raced off to the yurt and returned with a wooden box. Dodie stood by and watched as the yellow liquid was poured down Axel's throat. He found himself holding his breath until the antidote started to take effect. Axel's breathing slowed and soon his coughing subsided.

"What did you eat?" questioned Oban.

Axel shook his head. "Only what you gave me."

"Did the food ever leave your sight before you ate it?"

"No, no," panted Axel. "I took it from you and ate it right away."

"And you drank only water from the well?"

Axel nodded.

Dodie's eyes widened. "Axel set down his cup of water for a minute. I thought I saw Nye from Alsta do something behind him. I thought I saw a little glass bottle."

"Find Nye from Alsta!"

Two officials fanned out to find the racer. Bae returned with a cup of water and offered it to Axel, but he pushed the water away. Suddenly they heard excited voices at a campfire on the other side of the yurt. Dodie expected to see the officials return with Nye in shackles, but they came back empty-handed.

"He was clean," reported one.

"Really?" asked Dodie in disbelief. "I'm sure he poisoned Axel."

"Perhaps yes, perhaps no. Without evidence, we can't disqualify him. Best watch out for him."

"Will Axel be okay?" Dodie looked down at his kinsman who in the warm firelight looked green.

Oban shook his head. "Axel is not safe until he passes the poison completely. He must drink the antidote every hour until the poison leaves his body. I'm afraid the race is over for him."

Axel groaned, but couldn't find the strength to argue. Randi and Bae gave him farewell pats on the shoulders. The officials lifted Axel and carried him into their yurt where they would nurse him back to health.

Dodie ran back to his campsite where he found Zinnia awake.

"What happened?" she asked.

Dodie told her about Axel and his suspicion that Nye was the poisoner.

"You've got another suspect, then" said Zinnia. "Nye was at the Magistrate's feast, right? I wouldn't put it past him to do something horrible like poison Taj. He's not to be trusted, believe me."

"He's from your village, right? You know him well?"

"I wish I didn't." Zinnia turned Dodie's hour glass over. "Your turn to sleep."

Dodie laid down and soon fell into a dreamless sleep.

Chapter 8

"*Psst!* Wake up."

Dodie snapped awake and sat up, blinking around at the dying campfire, his rolled up racer rug, and the masked face peering close to his. Then he remembered where he was.

"It's your turn to watch," Zinnia whispered as she laid her head on her rolled up carpet.

"Right." Dodie scooted closer to the low flames, feeling the coldness of impending dawn.

The sky was changing from black to deep blue, and the stars were losing their vibrancy. The moon was westward bound, and soon the sun would be chasing away all remnants of the night. Dodie would feel better once daylight came, for now that the campfires were dying out, the shadowy lumps of bodies sleeping looked creepy. He had never been a fan of the darkness, and he often had vivid dreams that made him cry out in his sleep. Taj was always there to wake him from his nightmares and remind him he was fine. Taj made him feel safe, but right now Taj was far away, trapped in his own nightmare. Dodie shuddered.

He passed the next hour refreshing his memory of the Grand Flyer course for the second day. He held the map close to the weak firelight. Today the course would take him northeast across the Dead Lands where the terrain turned from sandy to rocky. Right after the first noon-day pit stop, he would race through a steep canyon called Quillian's Pass. By the looks of it, getting through the canyon would take up most of the day, then the checkpoint was just on the northern side. Dodie didn't think it would be too dangerous, but he had already underestimated the course yesterday.

Next he unrolled his grandfather's secret map, after making sure no one was awake yet, and checked it for any clues to navigating the day's course. Sure enough there were a few small sketches of rocks and the canyon, and a few notes scrawled next to them: *Abbra-Kadabbra for protection,* said one note. Another note said, *Refuge Q.* Right now these made no sense, but Dodie made a mental note for later. As the eastern sky glowed with rosy light, Oban emerged from the large yurt and headed over to Dodie.

"Good morning," he greeted in a whisper, his face beaming with excitement again. He handed the boy a clay bowl of yogurt sprinkled with cinnamon, a cup of steaming coffee, and a wedge of pita bread. "You have permission to take off as soon as you're ready. Dawn is nearly upon us. Good luck!"

Dodie used the pita bread like a spoon to eat the yogurt. He washed down the bread with the coffee, which warmed and energized him. He tied on his sandals, pulled on his head mask, secured his waist pouch behind him, and picked up *Phoenix*. He stood for a moment over Zinnia, watching her sleep, then bent down and nudged her softly.

She grunted and rolled over.

"I have to take off," Dodie whispered. "You gonna be okay?"

"Fine." Zinnia sounded a little grumpy.

"Maybe I'll see you at the pit stop. Good luck." Dodie carried his rug on his shoulder and picked his way around the other racers who were stirring.

At the edge of the camp, he mounted his carpet. He could see better now that the sky was lightening, and he checked his compass to be sure he was heading in a northeast direction. Lastly, he rummaged around behind him in his waist pouch and found a small vial of Binni's bright pink potion. He wanted to take the dose as late as possible so it would last as long as possible that day. If he took it too early before sunrise it might not last until sunset. The other racers were now awake, stretching and yawning and eating their breakfast. He had to leave now if he wanted to make the most of his head start. He uncorked the vial, and choked down the bitter potion, which bubbled as it slid down his throat. He tossed the empty vial into the sand, and gripped the braided loops on his carpet.

With barely a thought, he shot off into the pink sky. He shivered slightly in the cool morning air, and guided *Phoenix* lower to where the air was not quite so fresh. Soon the checkpoint was too tiny to see, and vast desert engulfed his vision. The sun rose, and Dodie wondered who would be first behind him. It wouldn't be Axel, that much he knew.

He was sure Nye had poisoned Axel's water, and wondered if he had any connection to Taj's poisoning. Maybe over the next two days Dodie would be able to discover the perpetrator. How great would it be to not only return to Turah the victor of the Grand Flyer and the savior of his family, but also the discoverer of the culprit?! Whatever happened, he prayed justice would be served.

Dodie felt exhilarated, partly from the beautiful blue sky, vibrant reddish dunes, and crisp air washing over him as he flew. But mainly he felt exhilarated by the desire—no, the *need*—to win this race.

With no one else nearby, he enjoyed his early morning flight, and experimented with different moves on *Phoenix*. He practiced a few nose dives and quick pull ups to avoid hitting the ground. He swooped from side to side, and zig-zagged. Although there were no walls in his path to practice on, he went through the motions of threading. He was able to keep his balance and bring *Phoenix* almost completely sideways. He knew it was much trickier to fly this way inches from a wall without snagging on it, but he felt more confident knowing he could get into a threading position. It also helped that no one was around to watch him.

By late morning, the landscape had changed from sandy desert to rocky terrain as he entered the Dead Lands. Here and there columns of red rock spiked up from the ground, and boulders as large as houses defended the earth. Dodie had to watch his flight path more carefully, for a few times he narrowly missed running into a tall rock column or outcrop. As the morning wore on, the temperature rose. The sun's heat radiated off the rocky terrain. There was still no sign of any racers, and Dodie was feeling good . . .

. . . Until he sighted something strange below him. Carved into the side of a rocky hill was what looked like the front of an ancient temple. The face of the rock was smooth and ornately decorated with molding and scroll work. A small open doorway stood at the foot of the hill. This rocky hill with its carved face stood directly on the race course.

Dodie slowed as he neared it, for he had a feeling of foreboding. He remembered the sketch of a rock on his grandfather's map and wondered if this was it. Halting and hovering in mid-air, he fished out the secret map to check it again. The sketch of the rock was labeled merely *Tomb* with the note *Abbra-Kadabbra for protection*.

Stuffing the map away in his waist pouch, Dodie continued on toward the tomb. The wind was gustier, and Dodie had to hold on tightly as he started to slowly pass over the rocky hill with its tomb.

"Help! Please, someone help me!" a voice rang out from the boulders below.

Dodie pulled up quickly and searched below him. He spied the figure of a man standing outside the tomb, waving his arms madly up at him.

Squinting against the wind, Dodie studied the figure, and to his astonishment recognized him as Petra, Magistrate Oxard's son who had raced and disappeared in the Grand Flyer five years ago. Dodie could recognize him from his shaved head and the serpent tattoo on his forearm. He was surprised that Petra didn't look a day older from when he raced five years ago, and he had somehow managed to keep his head shaved in the desert.

"Help! I need your help! *Please!*" Petra screamed up to him.

Everyone assumed Petra had died in the race, and his family had held burial services for him back in Turah. Had he been hiding out in the tomb all these years? Dodie dove down.

Petra stopped waving as Dodie neared him. He wore a smile that was not entirely friendly. Dodie wasn't quite sure what was amiss, but his spine tingled at the sight of the missing racer. He kept his distance a few feet above Petra's shiny head.

"We thought you were dead," said Dodie, unsure how to greet someone who everyone thought was, well, dead.

Petra's face twitched peculiarly, and Dodie wondered if living alone in the desert for five years hadn't addled his mind a bit.

"No, no, I'm quite alive," Petra said with a raspy voice, this time flashing a grin that was borderline sinister-looking.

Dodie gained another foot of height. Petra flinched.

"You should return home," Dodie told him.

"I have no carpet, or I would have long ago. Let me ride with you."

Dodie shook his head. "Sorry, I'm racing."

Petra's glassy eyes lit up with a glimmer. "So there will be more racers coming by here after you?" He licked his bottom lip quickly.

"Yeah, I'm the first one." Dodie was feeling down right uneasy now. "I must go." He started to sail away.

"*No! Wait!*" Petra screamed in desperation.

Dodie jerked to a stop, caught off-guard by the anguish in Petra's voice.

Petra was on his knees. "At least take a letter for me to my family so they'll know I'm alive and where I am. *Please!*"

Reluctantly, Dodie swooped over to Petra. The young man's eyes locked onto Dodie and his face hardened.

"Where's your letter?" asked Dodie, a few feet away.

Petra reached inside his tunic and held out a small scroll of paper. "Come closer."

Slowly, Dodie drifted nearer to him and reached

out his hand to take the scroll.

The scroll evaporated into air. Quick as a flash, Petra clasped an iron grip around Dodie's wrist.

"Petra!" Dodie stopped short.

It wasn't Petra.

First the eyes changed from glassy brown to glowing red. Starting with the feet, the human body was transforming in a swirl of dark mist that reeked of death. The long muscular legs lost their leggings and became gray bony limbs. Next, the torso shriveled into a rib cage. The whole body lost its clothing and muscle, and was reduced to a skeletal frame with sagging gray hide. The face was the worst part. The ears grew pointed ends, the nose curled out into a hook, and the mouth growled with yellow, razor-sharp teeth.

Dodie stared in shock, unable to pull his wrist free, unable to will his carpet to flee, unable to even scream.

"Thank ye, thank ye for stopping, kind sir,
You've given a ghoul a meal, as it were.
No fuss, no quarrel, is the best way to go,
I feast quickly to help ease your woe."

The ghoul spoke in a raspy voice, his breath rotten with decay. He started to tow Dodie, still kneeling on *Phoenix*, toward the open tomb. He hunched to one side and limped, wheezing heavily as if from great exertion.

Dodie mastered his senses, and pulled his arm hard. Despite his weak appearance, the creature held tightly.

"Let me go!" shouted Dodie, starting to panic as

the ghoul dragged him and *Phoenix* closer to the tomb.

The ghoul did not turn around as he replied,

"My grip is a shackle you cannot break,
I have no heart for you to wake,
There is no way to raise alarm,
For I am magical and cannot be harmed."

Dodie was pulled through the dark doorway. Blackness enveloped him and he could see nothing in the tomb except for the ghoul's glowing red eyes that glared at him hungrily. Dodie pulled and pulled, but could not break free. The ghoul inhaled a long deep draft of air. Dodie felt lightheaded. A force in the core of his being was pulling toward the ghoul like a magnet.

He also felt pain. Sharp pain. It was as if his insides were being sucked out of him. His good luck charm also seared his skin beneath his tunic. Dodie was on the verge of blacking out. He felt helpless, hopeless. How could he escape this dark magic?

Magic! Of course!

Suddenly, Dodie knew what to do, if only he could muster the strength to do it.

The ghoul inhaled. Dodie's life escaped him.

"Abbra-kadabbra!" Dodie screamed with all his might.

There was a flash of silver light, then an unearthly ear-splitting shriek, then Dodie was free from the ghoul's grasp and inhaling pull. He shot out of the tomb and up into the safety of the sky. Panting, he stopped *Phoenix* in midair. He sprawled on his back, taking in deep breaths and rubbing his chest where he had felt his insides being ripped from him. Then he peered over the edge of his carpet. Down below outside the tomb's entrance, the ghoul had reclaimed the form of Petra and was waving, but not at him. Dodie followed the ghoul's gaze, and spotted flying dots on the horizon. The other racers were catching up.

Most of the racers ignored the disguised ghoul who was frantically trying to get their attention. One racer, on a burgundy rug, swooped down for a closer look. This time the ghoul wasted no time on conversation. He leaped up and sprang onto the racer's back, all the while transforming back into his ghoulish form. The racer screamed in terror, trying to fight off the predator on his back. They disappeared into the tomb.

Dodie shuttered as he searched the sky for Zinnia. Suddenly, a figure ran out of the tomb. It was the racer who had just been attacked.

"I escaped!" the racer yelled, running away from the tomb. "Help!"

Before Dodie could respond, another racer flying a teal rug dove down to rescue his kinsman.

"What the—" Dodie watched the supposed victim turn into the ghoul and attack the new racer on the teal rug.

"That's what ghouls do," Zinnia shouted as she raced up alongside Dodie. "They take the form of their last victim to lure more victims. They feed on human souls."

"So Petra was his last victim," mumbled Dodie.

"You didn't stop for him, did you?"

"Well, I . . . uh . . ."

"You *did?*" Zinnia's eyes widened behind her mask. "How did you escape? No one can escape a ghoul!"

Dodie rubbed his chest again. "Let's just say I know a little magic."

"Well, I underestimated you, Rue," Zinnia said. With that last remark, she sped off in a northeast direction.

Two other racers followed her as more appeared on the horizon.

"Idiot!" Dodie yelled at himself for lingering too long. "Let's fly!"

Phoenix zoomed away from the tomb, the screams below soon fading in the distance. He noticed Zinnia, Atallah, and Nye up ahead. Atallah was showing off by weaving in between the tall rock columns. Nye kept trying to close the gap between himself and Zinnia. Behind Dodie, the remaining racers struggled to catch up.

It was almost noon, so Dodie kept his eyes peeled for the pit stop. Already he could see the hazy outline of Quillian's Pass miles ahead. As he climbed up over a large boulder and surfed down the other side, he saw the pit stop. A yurt was stationed beside a still pool of water, the rocks, clouds, and blue sky reflected in its tranquil waters. Zinnia, Atallah, and Nye skidded to a stop, and Dodie was not far behind.

"How stupid can you be?" Atallah was saying loudly. "You think some racer from the past is gonna camp out in a tomb all this time? It was *obviously* a ghoul." He yanked off his head mask and knelt beside the shallow pool.

Dodie hopped of *Phoenix* and joined Zinnia by the pool. She took her sandals off and dipped her small feet into the water. Dodie noticed Nye watching her closely, particularly her feet, and he elbowed her.

"What?" She looked at him.

"Your feet might give you away," he whispered to her.

Zinnia caught Nye studying her, and hastily tied her sandals back on.

Dodie pulled off his mask, knelt down, and lapped up water with his hand. The water was cool and sweet, and he drank more.

"How did we catch up to you, Rat Scat?" Atallah took a drink. "You stopped for the ghoul, didn't you?" He chuckled.

"Mind your own business," said Dodie, straightening up.

Atallah glared at him. "You still haven't thrown up. What's the deal?"

Dodie ignored him and lapped up more water.

"Well, whatever's the deal, you're only as good as your tricks." Atallah tied his sandals back on. "And no one can win this race on tricks alone. You don't belong here. You belong down on the ground in the alleys catching rats. And that's where you'll stay after my father owns you and your family. Except for Taj, cuz he'll be dead."

Dodie snapped, and charged at Atallah. He head-butted him in the stomach, and knocked him to the rocky ground. It took Atallah a moment to recover his surprise, which allowed Dodie an opportunity to punch him in the jaw. But then Atallah fought back and Dodie didn't stand a chance because Atallah was quick and strong. He pinned Dodie down and repeatedly punched him in the face, the chest, and the shoulders.

"Cut it out!" Zinnia screamed, forgetting to hide her high voice. No one heeded her.

The other racers encircled the two fighters on the ground, whooping and clapping.

Dodie curled up in a ball and covered his head with his arms. He was no match for Atallah.

Finally, Atallah stopped, tired and sweaty. He straightened up and sniffed.

"Rat Scat," he muttered, dabbing his bloody lip where Dodie had hit him. He strode off to the yurt in search of food.

The other racers dispersed to grab food and water.

Gingerly, Dodie got to his feet and stumbled over to the pool where he checked his reflection in the still water. His jaw was swelling, his nose was bleeding, and his cheek bones already had bruises. He groaned and softly bathed his face. He avoided looking at Zinnia when she came up beside him.

"So that was stupid," she muttered.

Dodie snorted, then winced. "Yeah, really stupid."

"He said some pretty low things."

Dodie didn't say anything.

Zinnia reached into her waist pouch and handed him a tiny jar. "This'll help."

Dodie used his finger to rub the creamy ointment into his wounds. He immediately felt the achiness, stinging, and throbbing begin to lessen. He gave the jar back to her. "That stuff's amazing. You get it from an alchemist?"

Zinnia tucked the ointment back in her waist pouch. "It's an old family potion."

Together they quickly grabbed food from the yurt, more bread and bananas, and ate. The other racers were already unrolling their carpets. Dodie took one more drink of water, then mounted *Phoenix*. He tried not to groan as he pulled on his facemask. His whole body was feeling sore. He hoped the next few miles to Quillian's Pass would be smooth so he could recover more. His ribs hurt when he tucked his knees under him, so he lay flat on his belly. He made an easy takeoff, not wanting to get jerked around by a sudden one.

Zinnia was right: fighting Atallah was stupid.

Chapter 9

"A little wager, gentlemen?" Atallah was buzzing around the other racers as they ate up the miles across the Dead Lands.

"What did you have in mind?" Nye called out in a deep voice.

"A race to Quillian's Pass," replied Atallah, gliding alongside Nye. "First one to reach the opening gets a five second head start into it. Everybody in?"

Several nodded their assent.

Dodie moaned. He did not feel like racing—wait, they were already doing that! But he wasn't about to be the only racer not man enough to agree.

"Everybody line up!" ordered Atallah.

The racers, still flying through the air, edged into position side by side. Dodie took the end place farthest away from Atallah. He wanted to avoid any unnecessary contact as best he could because he wasn't feeling too great. The sun was at its peak, blazing high in the hazy blue sky, and there was no breeze to counter the heat. Billowing clouds were moving in like a thick blanket overhead, trapping everything in a humid covering. The rocky landscape gave off a visual temperature, making the heat feel more intense than it might have been. Dodie's tunic was soaked through, and he wanted to rip off his head mask. His face was throbbing in the places where Atallah's fist had connected, and he wished he could apply more of Zinnia's ointment. Removing his head mask was a risky move with sand, bugs, and small pebbles on the loose, so he gritted his teeth and tried to hone in on the canyon a few miles ahead.

"It's on!" shouted Atallah.

Everyone blasted off. Being this was the first time all the racers had all started at the exact same time, Dodie found it interesting to assess them all. Three racers from the eastern village of Bruna immediately fell behind— not due to their lack of skill, but to the poor quality of their racer rugs. Dodie felt some family pride when he noticed that the racer rugs purchased from Rue's Rug Emporium had shot into the lead.

He kept his distance from the other racers as many started to employ some dangerous moves. Nye streaked past a racer like a bolt of lightning, his black and red carpet scathing the racer's head, which sent the racer toppling off his carpet to the earth below. Dodie looked back to watch the racer slam into a towering rock column, bounce off a few feet, then crash to the stony ground. Dodie cringed, doubting the racer had survived.

Dodie felt more confident as *Phoenix* effortlessly moved into the lead without him having to do much. The other racers noticed this. Out of the corner of his eye, Dodie saw Atallah speeding closer to him.

"Curses," Dodie muttered under his breath.

Phoenix's speed alone wouldn't be enough. He had to apply some skill, but the trouble was he had few tricks in his bag.

"Let's see whatcha got!" Atallah crowed as he narrowed the gap between their carpets, then dipped hard to the left.

Dodie recognized the move—Atallah was going to thread him. Dodie leaned sideways to the right. The undersides of their carpets touched as they tried to thread on each other. Dodie held his position as they zoomed on together, then he felt a push. Atallah was trying to force him downward. Dodie pushed back.

He knew if Atallah gained just a few more inches of elevation it would be over. He felt Atallah's carpet rise, so he rose with him. Atallah started to level out, trying to crush down on him. Dodie felt himself leaning back, and knew he was dangerously close to turning upside-down. He could feel his knees losing contact with his rug.

He hated retreating from Atallah, but it was better than falling off his carpet. He would have to pull back, and let Atallah take the lead. Dodie growled in frustration.

He was about to pull his carpet up when he saw another solution ahead. A rock column stood directly in their path. Atallah would have to break free.

He heard Atallah curse as they rushed toward the rock tower. Feet before hitting it, the two carpets peeled apart, *Sky Cleaver* veering left and *Phoenix* careening right.

The quick split was all Dodie needed. He cleared the rock mast and coaxed a burst of speed from *Phoenix*. To his surprise, he noticed that he and Atallah were still in the lead.

Atallah kept glancing at Dodie, his eyes narrowed. Dodie, for his part, wanted to take control and attack Atallah, but he lacked the confidence, so he merely sped ahead and kept a watchful eye on his opponent.

Quillian's Pass was fast approaching now, and the opening looked narrower than Dodie had anticipated. It was more like a crack in the mountain side, big enough for only one racer at a time to go through. Dodie was imagining all the racers crowding to get into the canyon when he suddenly noticed how close Atallah had come to him. He was so close Dodie could smell his sweat. He braced himself for Atallah's next move.

Atallah suddenly kicked out his leg to the side.

Phoenix responded before Dodie did, and rolled up her side to deflect the kick. This gave Dodie a chance to swerve away, but in doing so, Atallah took the lead and blasted into the canyon first. Dodie came to a sharp stop just outside the narrow opening.

Atallah cruised around to face him a few feet inside the canyon. "I win! Remember, it's a five second head start! No cheating or you'll be sorry. Nice flying with you, Rat Scat!" He laughed, turned around, and disappeared behind a boulder.

Dodie counted. *One . . . two . . .*

Nye pulled up behind him.

. . . three . . .

Next came Zinnia.

. . . four . . .

As more racers arrived, they all looked around at each other, thinking the same thing: who would be next to enter Quillian's Pass?

"Five!" yelled Dodie.

Nye spun like a top, causing everyone to back away. Then he streaked through the narrow opening and disappeared.

Dodie and Zinnia wasted no more time, barreling past the other racers and into the canyon. Dodie stayed ahead one carpet distance from Zinnia. He was impressed with his own aggressiveness.

For the first few miles, Quillian's Pass was too narrow for passing, forcing the racers to fly single-file. The canyon walls loomed high enough to block the sun and cast shadows. The ground below was a dry riverbed, and sharp boulders jutted out here and there, creating a precarious obstacle course. Dodie started to feel a little claustrophobic, especially with the thickening cloud cover sealing him in overhead. Atallah was nowhere in sight, and Nye was several yards ahead. At this rate, they both would likely clear the Pass and arrive at the checkpoint first. At least Dodie was next in line with Zinnia riding his tail.

Randi tried to pass Zinnia a few times by going higher or lower, but each time she matched his move and blocked him from passing her. Dodie wondered if she would try to pass him. A few minutes later she did just that. She rose a few feet above him, trying to pass overhead, but he jetted up and blocked her. He thought he heard her giggle, and he chuckled.

"Something's gotta give soon," Zinnia told him. "I'm getting tired of riding your butt."

Dodie grinned. "Get used to it!"

"I saw you threading with Atallah. Not bad."

"Thanks." Dodie felt a tickle of pleasure—she had been watching him. "You're not bad yourself."

"I know," she was quick to reply. "No offense, but I'm better than you."

"Let's see," Dodie barked as he increased his speed.

Ahead the canyon started to widen just a little. Dodie waited for Zinnia to make her next move as he let her edge up beside him.

He leaned sideways. By now he was feeling more comfortable with threading, and he gave her no time to respond. With his right hand, he shoved her out of the way, and heard her give a surprised yelp. He glanced back, saw she was okay, and took a large lead as the Pass narrowed again.

They didn't speak to each other for the next hour.

As they flew on and on, Dodie was growing weary with the scenery, and wondered how much longer he had to fly trapped in this canyon. He was not the only one feeling this way, for the other racers looked less tense. Randi was sitting up on his knees with one hand gripping his loop. Behind him, Bae stretched out on his belly, while another racer sat cross-legged and dug in his waist pouch for his compass. Dodie's legs were stiff and his back ached. He really wanted to stretch, but he couldn't afford losing his position. Plus he didn't want to give Zinnia another reason to think less of him.

Dodie's eyes wandered around, and he noticed several openings in the canyon walls that he took to be caves. He was surprised to see them marked with rugged Qs carved into the stone, and he remembered the note on his grandfather's secret map: *Refuge Q.*

In the late afternoon, the weather rapidly changed. Dark, fast moving clouds made the sky gray and the sunlight dull, but did not lessen the heat. A gusty wind suddenly picked up from the south and whistled up through Quillian's Pass. Everyone readjusted his position and braced himself against the wind. Dodie detected a faint rumbling sound behind him in the distance that was gradually growing louder. He had no idea what it was. Thunder perhaps? The wind grew stronger, blowing sand and debris, and Dodie had to squint against the dust. The rumbling sound was getting closer to them.

"Sand storm!" Randi cried from behind.

Dodie turned just in time to see the racer at the very end of the line get swallowed by a sandy cloud. He couldn't believe what he was seeing. A thick wall of sand was rushing through the canyon straight after them. It was traveling at an incredible speed, and devouring everything in its path. Its force was sucking the racers back into its grasp. Two more racers got whipped backward and disappeared into the cloud.

"We can't outrun it!" Zinnia screamed behind him.

Dodie started to panic until he spotted a Q carved above an opening up ahead on his right. "Follow me!"

The sand storm took out Bae, and was fast approaching.

Dodie held on, and struggled to keep his speed. He felt the wind sucking him from behind. *Phoenix* quivered.

"Grab hold of *Phoenix*!" Dodie ordered Zinnia. "Do it!"

Zinnia grabbed one of *Phoenix's* back tassels. *Phoenix* lurched with the extra weight. Dodie kept his eyes on the Q ahead. Almost there. Zinnia shrieked, the sand storm right behind her.

"Ahhh!" Dodie dove into the hole marked with the Q.

Seconds later the sand storm tore by, engulfing the canyon in a dark swirling cloud.

Chapter 10

Dodie braked suddenly, causing Zinnia to ram into him from behind. For a moment, they sat on their hovering carpets, panting heavily. Dodie could feel Zinnia's heart thumping on his back as she leaned on him. He was sorry his back was sweaty, but he liked having her so close. She started laughing, her voice a little shaky, and she slowly sat up.

Dodie turned around to face her. "What's so funny?"

Zinnia pulled off her head mask, her face glistening with sweat. Dodie had almost forgotten what she looked like—he hadn't seen her without her mask since first crashing into her. She was prettier than he remembered, with large brown eyes and thick lashes.

"How in the world did you know there was a cave here?" She looked shocked.

Dodie gingerly peeled off his head mask and attempted a grin, but his face was too sore. "None of your business."

Zinnia laughed again and scooted off her rug. *Amethyst* rolled up.

Dodie did the same and stretched his arms high. "Ouch." His hands scraped the rocky ceiling of the cave.

With the foggy light from outside, he could just make out the ceiling, but could not see how deep the cave went. He joined Zinnia at the opening to watch the sand storm rage outside.

"How long d'ya think the storm will last?" he asked.

Zinnia shrugged. "Sand storms are unpredictable. Could be minutes or hours." She sat down and leaned against the wall.

"How come you know so much?" Dodie asked as he plopped down across from her and leaned against the wall. "About ghouls and sand storms and potions."

Zinnia smiled. "I used to live abroad. My father was a traveling alchemist."

"Was?" Dodie prodded.

Zinnia gazed out at the storm. "A few months ago he disappeared. He went on a business trip to the Capital, but never made it there. I went looking for him along the route he had traveled, but I could find no sign of him."

"Do you think . . . your father's . . ."

"Dead?" Zinnia met his gaze. "I'm choosing to believe he's still alive. I've already lost my mother, I can't think about losing my father."

Dodie nodded. "My mother died, too. It's always

been just me and my dad and grandpapa and brother."

Before he could stop himself, he rambled on about how his father was constantly stressed about the business and hardly there; and how his grandfather was crippled and did his best to hide his deep sadness over it; and how his brother always looked out for him and made him feel less bad about being afraid of flying. Here he bit his lip, but Zinnia immediately pried about this. He relented and told her about Binni's potion—which she found fascinating, being an alchemist's daughter and all. Dodie quickly turned the conversation back to Zinnia's father.

"My father was a very skilled alchemist, and he knew many secrets. He was always either in high demand or in danger." Zinnia sighed. "I need him back."

Dodie brightened with understanding. "That's why *you're* racing. To wish for your father's return. But you can't wish for him to come back to life if he's . . ."

"I know the genie's rules!" snapped Zinnia. "But he's *not* dead. He's too valuable alive."

Dodie was quiet.

Zinnia's face softened. "I'm sorry about Taj, really. Losing family is the worst—especially when it's all you've got. Too bad the prize isn't two wishes so I could give you one to use when I win."

Dodie was surprised by this thought of generosity on her part, even though it could never happen. An awkward silence filled the air between them.

"Listen," Dodie spoke up. "One of us has got to

win—no one else. We've got the best reasons to win that wish and treasure. I say we help each other out against the other competition—especially against Atallah and Nye."

"No argument there," snorted Zinnia.

"Then tomorrow when it comes down to us," Dodie swallowed, "may the best man win. Waddaya say?"

"Deal." Zinnia stuck out her hand.

Dodie gripped it, liking how small it was, yet it felt just as rough as his from gripping the braided loops on her carpet.

Zinnia dug in her waist pouch and tossed him the tiny jar of ointment. "Your face needs more."

Dodie caught the ointment and dabbed his wounds with it. "Feels much better, thanks." He dabbed a bit more on his chest where his good luck charm had seared him during the ghoul's attack.

"What's that you're carrying?" Zinnia pointed to the charm.

Dodie pulled it out from under his tunic and held it up by its thread. "A good luck charm. Taj bought it for me." He slipped it back under his tunic, and added quickly, "I don't really believe in it."

"But it's like having a little piece of your brother with you," Zinnia said softly.

Dodie gave a small smile, then tossed the ointment back to her. "This ointment is one of your father's secrets, right?"

Zinnia nodded as she stowed the jar back in her

pouch. "Have you thought any more about who poisoned Taj?"

"I've been thinking a lot about Nye," Dodie shrugged. "I know Nye poisoned Axel. He must've destroyed the bottle so it couldn't be traced to him. He was at the Magistrate's Banquet, too."

Zinnia raked her fingers through her short black hair. "There's always Atallah."

"Why, because he's such a jerk?"

"He seems to really hate your guts and look down on your family."

Dodie wasn't going to tell her about his family's debt to Lord Hadi, and the wager Gamal had made with him—both of which were good motives for Hadi to poison Taj. He'd considered Atallah, but wondered where he could have gotten Devil's Kiss from if it was as rare as Raz claimed. Yet Atallah was rich and could probably afford to go to great lengths to buy it from another alchemist. Or maybe he paid Raz to acquire it for him. After all, he would need an alchemist's input on which deadly poison to use. Quite convenient that he chose a poison with an equally hard-to-get antidote. Dodie yawned, starting to feel very comfortable in the cool cave.

Furthermore, Dodie was still shocked that Raz was sponsoring Atallah. Binni was his best friend, and his father and Raz had been friends for years. He couldn't believe Raz didn't sponsor Taj! Why didn't he?

Dodie remembered what Binni had told him at the

Magistrate's Banquet: Raz knew something about Taj that made him go with Atallah.

Dodie kicked off his sandals.

He *knew* something . . .

Like maybe a prophecy! Very likely, especially since Raz and Atallah had been waiting outside the Seer's tent and could have overheard the prophecy—she was so darn loud.

Then he shook his head. No, Raz wouldn't try to kill Taj, but maybe Raz knew someone else, like Atallah, was going to take out Taj because of the prophecy, so he didn't sponsor Taj. He knew Taj would never race. Dodie made a mental note to ask Raz if anyone came to him seeking Devil's Kiss, or if he knew about anyone's plan to kill off Taj.

"Do you think the sand storm caught up to Nye and Atallah?" Zinnia's voice broke through his thoughts.

Dodie snapped his eyes back to her. "I sure hope so. I wouldn't mind if it finished them off, too. Atallah's convinced he's better than anyone else and has every girl in Turah pining for him because of his blue eyes."

Zinnia smirked. "I never noticed his eyes because he's so arrogant."

Dodie wanted to ask if she had anyone she was pining for back in Alsta, but he didn't think he could bear it if her answer was yes. Not now anyway. He guessed there had to be someone pining for her since she was pretty and smart and brave, but for now he didn't want to know.

"Hey, I think the storm is passing," he said as he looked out the opening. The sand was thinning so he could see the canyon outside.

"You're right." Zinnia crawled on her hands and knees and popped her head out. "We better get going."

They both mounted their carpets, pulled their head masks back on, and folded into the prostrate position. Dodie took the lead and sailed out of the cave, Zinnia right behind him. Behind them a few racers emerged from other caves bearing Qs. Dodie wondered how many had survived the storm.

"We better get a move on," urged Dodie. "You wanna go first this time?"

"Thanks." Zinnia moved in front of him. "Keep up."

Dodie laughed. "I'll try."

They took off before the other racers could get in front of them. A few yards up they passed one racer stranded on a boulder, his carpet nowhere in sight. He shook a fist up at them. They came up to Bae who had survived the storm. Blood seeped through his head mask and he was flying in a wobbly way. As they rode his tail, he turned back to them.

"Go ahead and pass me," he said weakly. "I've gotta take it easy for a while. That storm almost finished me off."

"Sorry," said Dodie, and he meant it. He followed Zinnia over Bae's injured head.

"Dodie, look ahead!" said Zinnia.

Dodie craned his neck to look around her. A few yards ahead of them he saw Atallah and Nye flying close together.

"They must've gotten slowed down by the storm," Zinnia said excitedly. "Let's see if we can get close enough to eavesdrop."

They sailed up behind the two racers. Atallah was in the lead, flying casually, as Nye trailed him, not making any move to pass.

"I'm telling you," Atallah's bawdy voice rang off the rocks, "he couldn't fly a foot and now he's racing. Something's up."

"Maybe he's taking a tonic," suggested Nye in his deep voice. "Alchemists can come up with anything."

"Believe me, I know what alchemists are capable of," Atallah said darkly.

"There's something going on with him and Zin," grunted Nye. "They said Zin's from my village, but I'd don't think I know him. If he'd just take his mask off, maybe I could tell who he is!"

Zinnia smiled in satisfaction upon hearing this.

"Yeah, why won't he take off his mask?" Atallah wondered. "Something's up with him, too. I'm gonna get to the bottom of all this."

"Maybe we'll get lucky and someone will poison them both," said Nye in an amused voice.

Atallah chortled. "Yeah, maybe *someone* will."

"Like you?" Dodie couldn't help hollering, his voice echoing off the high canyon walls.

Without looking back, Atallah called, "You survived, huh? You're cheating somehow. No one with no flying experience could possibly survive as long as you have."

"There aren't too many ways to cheat in this race," Dodie reminded him. "There aren't that many rules. Anything goes."

Atallah snorted. "You're right, anything goes. Right, Nye?"

"Right."

Atallah reached behind him and grabbed one of Nye's front tassels. Nye scooted completely around so he was riding backwards and facing Zinnia. Then he reached into his waist pouch, and chucked something tiny at Zinnia. It was too small to duck from. There was a loud *snap-crack*, then a small spark landed on Zinnia's arm and ignited. She shrieked and hastily patted her arm to put out the little flame. Nye eyed her suspiciously, obviously surprised by her girlish squeal. His wrist flicked at her again.

Snap-crack!

The spark landed on her carpet and caught her front tassel. She scrambled to put it out.

Nye chucked one over Zinnia's head at Dodie, but his aim was off and the spark extinguished on a passing boulder.

"Pull back!" Dodie yelled to Zinnia.

They both slowed, and watched Atallah and Nye zoom off amidst howls of laughter.

"What *was* that?" Zinnia gasped. "I thought magic carpets are fire-proof. The dragons couldn't burn us."

"They are," confirmed Dodie, "except against fire with magical properties. Nye definitely has a connection with an alchemist—a very powerful one. We better hang back."

"I guess it's better to be safe than first at checkpoint tonight," grumbled Zinnia.

They kept a few yards between themselves and Atallah and Nye.

The sun was no longer visible in the sky, for it was lowering in the west. The clouds had cleared, and the wind had died down. The towering canyon walls shaded them, and blocked their view of the sun in the west, but they were able to tell by the purple hue of the sky that sunset was starting. Soon the Pass widened and they could see the end a few miles in the distance. Atallah and Nye were far ahead, racing neck in neck to the checkpoint. Dodie rode beside Zinnia, keeping an eye on the other racers behind him.

Suddenly, Dodie felt queasy. He felt himself swaying, even though *Phoenix* was flying steady. There wasn't much in his stomach, but he wanted to throw up. He made the mistake of looking down, and his eyes crossed. He was still a ways from the checkpoint, and knew it was only a matter of minutes before Binni's potion had completely worn off.

"You okay?" Zinnia asked beside him.

"No," Dodie croaked. "Potion's run out."

"Take some more."

"I . . . can't . . ." Dodie groaned, closing his eyes for a minute, but that seemed to make him sicker. "I've got one more dose . . . for tomorrow."

"Get your mind off it," Zinnia told him. "Come closer." She reached out her hand and grabbed *Phoenix's* front tassel. "I've got you. Breathe and try to relax. Push past your fear."

Dodie put his head down on his carpet and inhaled and exhaled deeply and slowly. That was helping.

"Fix your eyes on something constant," Zinnia instructed.

Dodie turned his head and locked his eyes on her. Everything around him went out of focus as he kept his gaze on her. His stomach settled down. He pulled off his head mask, and felt the refreshing evening breeze. His hands stopped shaking.

"You're great at flying," said Zinnia, keeping her eyes ahead. "I think you could overcome your fear with some time."

"I've actually been enjoying it," Dodie admitted. "The Seer said someday I will overcome my fear—but I don't believe her. She also said Taj would be victorious."

"We're almost there—don't look ahead!" Zinnia warned when she noticed Dodie start to turn his head. "Keep your eyes on me!"

Dodie did as he was told, though he didn't need much persuasion. He kept breathing in and out, in and out, and kept staring at her.

Suddenly, they dropped and stopped. He lay a minute on his carpet and watched Zinnia dismount. Slowly, he lifted his head and saw the checkpoint before him and Quillian's Pass behind. In the west, the sun dipped below the horizon.

"Thanks," he told her. "I wouldn't have made it."

Zinnia smiled with her eyes. "We're in this together, right?"

Dodie smiled weakly and didn't know what to say.

Chapter 11

The checkpoint was a little oasis of palm trees clumped around a shallow pool of rainwater. A large bonfire lit the oasis, and one small yurt housed the five officials and provisions. By now, only six of the original twenty-five racers had made it: Dodie and Zinnia, Atallah and Nye, and Randi and Bae. Everyone else had either been lost in the sandstorm or had arrived at the checkpoint after sunset and been disqualified. A part of Dodie couldn't believe he was still in the running, and another part of him chided himself for doubting he could win this race. After all, he had no choice—he *had* to win this Grand Flyer.

The racers gathered around the bonfire, kicked off their sandals, pulled off their head masks, and hungrily devoured the baskets of chicken, pita bread, hummus, and dates. Of course Zinnia kept her mask on and sneaked bites behind it, despite Atallah's glares of suspicion. Dodie kept his eye on Atallah and Nye sitting across the bonfire from him and braced himself for a confrontation. His face was feeling better, but the thought of taking more swings made him cringe. Still, he was determined to protect Zinnia's secret.

The officials summoned Atallah for an interview with the Wishing Well since he had come in first to the checkpoint. Atallah strutted off.

After dinner, Dodie laid down, resting his head on his rolled up carpet, and felt very satisfied and sleepy. He gazed up at the sprinkle of stars winking between the palm fronds, and felt heavy drowsiness overtaking him. If he could just rest his eyes for a minute . . . he was so tired . . .

He heard a shuffle beside him and jolted awake. Zinnia plopped down on the sand.

"You falling asleep?" she asked quietly. "We won't get much tonight. Our last day starts at midnight."

"Midnight! I thought we always take off at dawn." Dodie propped himself up on his elbows to look at her.

Zinnia shook her head. "As if this race isn't hard enough, they gotta throw in racing in the dark."

"How do we stay on the course?" asked Dodie, his voice tight with panic. "How do we know which direction to fly without the sun?"

"Well, you can use your compass," Zinnia said with a patronizing look.

Dodie felt his cheeks turn red. "Oh, yeah, right."

"But it will be trickier," added Zinnia quickly. "And more dangerous. Especially with those two." She nodded toward Atallah and Nye who had their heads together in a hushed conversation. "We gotta stick together."

Dodie sat up and pulled out the race course map. By the firelight he saw the first leg of the race would be across a barren desert called the Phantom Plains, then the last leg to the Capital would be along the Siren Sea. He was excited about that part, for he had never seen the ocean.

Zinnia stood up. "I'm gonna get some water." She trudged over to the shallow pool by the yurt.

Hastily, Dodie fished out his grandfather's secret map and took a look. There was one note for the Phantom Plains (*Two are better than one*), but the coastal trek had two warnings: *heed not the siren's song,* and *hands off anything that shines*. As always, they didn't make much sense, but Dodie knew they would when he was in the moment of needing them.

"Why do you have two maps?" asked Zinnia as she returned.

Dodie started. "Oh, uh, just an extra race map."

Zinnia sat down next to him and leaned over to look at it. "So that's how you knew about those caves in the canyon."

"Do you think this is cheating?" he held up his grandfather's map.

Zinnia shrugged. "There are no rules. Can I see it?"

Dodie hesitated slightly, then handed it over.

Zinnia scooted closer to the firelight to study it.

"What've you got there?" called Atallah from the other side of the bonfire.

Dodie panicked. "I thought you were asleep."

"Never underestimate your opponent." Atallah stood up and started for them.

Dodie snatched the map from Zinnia and started stuffing it into his waist pouch, but Atallah was on him quicker than he expected. The two boys hit the sand, toppling over each other as one tried to steal the map and the other tried to protect it.

R-i-i-i-p-p!

"No!" cried Dodie as he broke away from Atallah, half the map in his fist.

Atallah stood panting, the other half of the map in his fist. Without even looking at it, he tossed it into the fire.

"What's wrong with you?!" screamed Dodie, smoke from the burning map stinging his eyes. "You're such a rat!"

"You're such a fraud!" Atallah shot back. "You gotta be put in your place—which should be no place at all in this race. I knew you couldn't be doing this on your own. Now you'll have to." He nodded at the charred remains of the map in the flames. "Go home to the rats." He returned to the other side of the bonfire.

Dodie plopped down next to Zinnia.

"I'm sorry," she whispered, lightly touching her shoulder to his.

"My grandfather gave me this map. It was his." He

fingered the scrap of dusty paper, then hid it away in his waist pouch. "I'll take the first watch. Get some sleep."

"You sure?" When he didn't answer, she lay down on her side facing him.

Dodie could feel her eyes on him as he stared into the blazing flames. A log snapped and he watched the sparks waft up to the sky. He wanted to talk with her—about what he didn't know—but she needed to sleep. As Zinnia drifted off, Dodie's thoughts drifted away.

He thought about her, wondering why he was so drawn to her. Maybe it was their mutual empathy for each other, having both lost their mothers and now both losing another dear family member—Taj and her father. Or maybe it was their desperation to win the Grand Flyer to save someone they loved. Dodie realized they had a lot in common, including the same fierce courage that prompted them both to enter a race they had no right to be in.

He thought about Taj. He was sad not only over Taj's fading life, but over Taj's missed chance to race in the Grand Flyer. For the past five years, Taj ate, slept, and breathed racing. He was physically designed for it with his long, lean frame and strength. And he was so good at it. Dodie imagined Taj whipping across the dunes, outrunning the sandstorm, and threading all over Atallah. Taj would have had the time of his life, and undoubtedly would have won the Grand Flyer. He would have saved the family from financial ruin and carried on the Rue racing legacy.

So unlike Dodie. Even if Dodie won, which would make his family more grateful than proud, he wouldn't be the Rue joining the racing legacy. Taj would have raced because it was in his blood and he wanted to. Dodie was racing because he *had* to. Sure, his secret dream had always been to be a racing Rue like his grandfather and his brother. Now he *was* racing, but he couldn't think of himself as a racer.

He felt like a fraud.

And he didn't need Atallah to point it out to him; he already knew it.

The only reason he was able to stay on a carpet was because of a pink potion. Without Binni's potion, he would still be the Rue who had a fear of flying. No, he couldn't call himself a proper racer, and racing would never be his thing.

He just had to win this one Grand Flyer, then he would go back to being the Rue everyone knew him to be. That was fine. At least he wouldn't have to catch rats for sheks anymore. The prize money would take care of that.

Dodie glanced at Zinnia who was asleep. He wondered if they would stay friends after the Grand Flyer, after they returned to their villages and he went back to being flightless. He wondered what she would say about him, if she would tell everyone about the potion he drank, or if she would be more generous and tell about how he got her back in the race with a stardust burst.

He sighed. He couldn't believe how selfish he was, worrying over Zinnia when his brother's life hung in the balance. He needed to keep his head in the game. He needed to win and wish for Taj's life.

Dodie stood up and stretched. He didn't like these thoughts in his head, even if he believed they were true. He suddenly felt down. He was exhausted, and his face was sore. He was worried about Taj. He wanted to be done. He just wanted everything to be all right again.

The other racers were asleep, so Dodie thought there would be no harm in leaving Zinnia for a minute to get a drink of water. He knelt by the pool and dipped his hand into the cool water. He cupped his hand to his mouth and sipped, and felt better.

He returned to Zinnia and let her sleep another two hours. He guessed it had to be around ten when he woke her.

"You let me sleep too long!" she hissed. "You're gonna get barely two hours of sleep."

"It's okay." Dodie lay down.

"You better not be dead weight on me."

"Don't worry." With a yawn, he was out.

He dreamed a collage of images. First, he dreamed of a man squatting in a corner of a dark and dirty room. He looked haggard and underfed. He poured a bright green liquid from a glass bottle into a clay bowl. Green smoke *poofed*. A cobra reared up from the bowl and slithered away.

Then he dreamed about the Seer. She sat rocking

back and forth, her body and face shrouded in black fabric. She raised her voice and cried,

"*You will triumph over both soul and body and have a change of heart.*

At journey's end you will be victorious and find more than you seek."

"It's almost midnight."

Dodie jerked awake, and sat up. He blinked at the lazy fire. Around him the other racers were strapping on their sandals and pulling on their head masks. Zinnia ignited *Amethyst.*

"Oh no," moaned Dodie.

"What's the matter?"

"My potion is only good for twelve hours."

"So?"

"If I take it now, it will wear off around noon. Will we be done with the race by then?"

"No, it goes till sunset. You only have one more dose?"

Dodie rolled his eyes. "I didn't know we'd be starting at midnight!"

"How were you planning on flying home without more?"

Dodie stared at her blankly. "Honestly, I haven't thought that far ahead. All I care about is saving Taj right now! And now I won't be able to!"

"Calm down. Take it now, and when it wears off I'll help you again."

"Then I *will* be dead weight! There's no way either

of us will win!"

"A lot can happen along the way," argued Zinnia. "You never know our luck—we could end up being the only two racers left at the end."

Dodie held his head in his hands. "I can't believe this!"

"Pull yourself together!" snapped Zinnia. "You still have one dose, and you still have your nerve. Don't think about it and just fly!"

Dodie took a deep breath. "Okay, okay." He dug out the small vial and gulped down the pink potion. He chucked the vial into the fire, then pulled on his head mask. "*Phoenix.*"

The magic carpet stretched out, her red, orange, and blue colors matching the fire, and her gold embellishments shining in the light. Dodie mounted the carpet and sailed to the edge of the oasis where the other racers had lined up. Apparently there had been no award for arriving first at this checkpoint, for both Atallah and Nye were still there. The five race officials stood on either end of the line of racers, their hands up in the air. Dodie and Zinnia parked on the end. Dodie bent over and gripped the braided loops. Ahead of him stretched the vast barren desert, blue and shadowy in the moonlight.

"You will reach a pit stop around dawn," one official told them. "And the last one around noon. Take heart, and may the best racer win."

The air was thick with tension as the racers watched

for the signal to go. All was still and silent.
At the same time, the officials dropped their arms.
The racers took off.

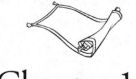

Chapter 12

There was something eerie about this desert, and it wasn't just because they were crossing it at night or because it was called the Phantom Plains. The moonlight cast a ghostly glow and spawned blue shadows along the dunes. The black sky glittered with stars, and the air was still. Normally it would be a beautiful setting—if it weren't for the creepy mood saturating the terrain. Several times Dodie felt his spine tingle and goose bumps prickle beneath his tunic, then abruptly they would go away for a few miles. He kept telling himself to calm down, stay focused, and stop reading into anything.

Everyone raced fairly, for the most part, and kept distance from each other. They were all bent on getting to the first pit stop, breathlessly awaiting the morning. Dodie noticed he was not the only one getting spooked. At one point Bae let out a shriek of surprise for what appeared to be no reason. Zinnia rubbed her arms, and

Dodie guessed she was feeling goose bumps. Dodie was just wondering what was wrong with this desert when he noticed something peculiar.

He happened to glance down below him, and saw a ripple in the sand following along with him. At first he figured it was the wind, but there was no wind—the air was stagnant. He barely felt a breath as he flew. He watched the ripple chase along below him.

He glanced over at the other racers, but saw no ripples chasing along below them. Was his carpet creating some sort of drag that was rippling the sand? He couldn't figure it out, but he felt goose bumps and a sort of coldness in his heart.

"What in the world?"

When he said these words, his breath made little pale puffs. The only time his breath ever did this was sometimes in the dead of winter when he would wake up in the middle of the night shivering. The air would be so dry and cold that his breath would emit puffs of smoke, as he called it. Taj usually let him share his bed for warmth since they couldn't afford extra oil for the heat lamps. Taj would always threaten Dodie that if he snored or drooled he had to go straight back to his own bed. Dodie guessed he never did either, for Taj never kicked him out.

Dodie's hands didn't feel abnormally cold, so he was surprised he could see his breath. The ripples below him started to grow, as if something hidden under the sand was surfacing. Dodie gripped his loops. He wasn't sure what he was expecting—another gigantic scorpion, or maybe a devilish spirit. He sure wasn't expecting what he saw next.

A sparkly arrow appeared in the sand, pointing ahead and speeding along below him. Dodie watched the arrow, his eyes transfixed on it. All sound around him grew muffled, including Zinnia's voice calling to him. He kept his eyes on the arrow below and followed it.

Then the arrow disappeared. Dodie slowed down a bit, his eyes searching below him for it. He looked ahead, and his heart leaped.

"Taj!" he yelled. "Taj! What are you doing here?"

His brother stood atop a sand dune, his tall, lean figure silhouetted against the blue moonlit sky. He did not wave or speak, but stared at Dodie.

Dodie was too excited to be confused at Taj's sudden appearance. He realized how much he had missed his brother over the past few days, and how desperately worried he was over his life. Seeing Taj standing there, tall and strong, caused a large lump to rise up in Dodie's throat.

"Taj! You have—no, wait! Where are you going?" Dodie raced ahead, but no matter how much sand he covered, he could get no closer to his brother. Taj always looked far away. Dodie wondered what was going on. Come to think of it . . .

How had Taj gotten here? Had he miraculously recovered, and gone in search of his little brother? Did this mean Dodie no longer had to race?

If only he could catch up to Taj. He could ask him these questions and invite him to hop on board *Phoenix*. He would give the reins over to Taj. After all, Taj was supposed to be crossing this desert right now— not Dodie. It would be such a relief to let Taj finish the race, and of course a relief not to worry about Taj's life anymore.

Taj disappeared. Dodie felt that lump flaring up in his throat again.

"No! Where are you? *TAJ!*" he screamed.

He crossed over the dune, and searched the horizon. There was no sign of Taj, not even footprints in the sand below. Dodie pulled up to a stop, sat up straight, and scanned the plains.

"You can't leave me. I *need* you." Dodie wiped his eyes and clutched the good luck charm strung around his neck.

He was all alone. He must have drifted off course from the other racers, for he had no idea where he was. He rummaged around behind him in his waist pouch and found his compass. He squinted at it in the darkness.

"Great!" he groaned.

North was behind him. He had veered completely south in the opposite direction of where he needed to go. But he couldn't turn around, not yet. He kept scanning the dunes for his brother. Maybe Taj would reappear. Dodie's eye caught a shadowing movement a few yards away, and he perked up, his heart beating with hope.

But the longer Dodie hovered there, he realized there was no Taj . . . there never had been. He couldn't explain what he had seen, but he knew it was beyond reason that his brother could be out there in the desert with him. Taj was hundreds of miles away, dying in his bed.

Turning *Phoenix* around, he zoomed off in a northern direction. He covered a few miles when suddenly Nye crossed his path, heading west. Dodie ignored him and kept going north.

Then he noticed the sand rippling below him.

"What *is* this?" Dodie muttered.

The glittering arrow appeared again. Dodie turned away from it, determined not to follow it, but it seemed the arrow was following him . . . until Dodie checked his compass. He was heading east.

"What?!" he growled. He adjusted his position.

He started to feel very muddled, for he couldn't tell if the arrow was following him for if he was following the arrow. Dodie tried to stay constant, but every time he checked his compass he found he had drifted off course. When he trained his eyes ahead, the arrow jumped ahead of him and took up his view. He grew frustrated.

Then he spotted another figure atop a distant sand dune. In the moonlight, he recognized his grandfather Nadar sitting on his carpet.

"Grandpapa!" Dodie waved at him. "I'm so glad to see you!"

Again Dodie took no time to question how his grandfather had managed to turn up there. He needed to see his grandfather's wrinkled face and hear his grandfather assure him he was doing the right thing by racing. He wanted to glean as many tips as possible about the Grand Flyer, and he was anxious to hear news on how Taj was doing.

But just as before, Dodie could never get any closer to Nadar. His grandfather, thin and hunched on his carpet, always appeared far away. Dodie gritted his teeth, determined to reach his grandfather.

"No—stay right there! Hey!"

Dodie coaxed more speed out of *Phoenix* to catch Nadar before he disappeared over the other side of the dune. He really needed his grandfather's encouragement right now. He was feeling alone and defeated, but there was no trace of Nadar.

Dodie fought back tears as he checked his compass, turned his carpet, and headed north again. He spotted Zinnia, which made him feel better, but then made him suspicious. Was this really Zinnia? Would she disappear like his brother and grandfather?

"There you are!" Zinnia called.

Dodie felt relief. "What's going on with this desert?"

"Mirages."

"You only see mirages when you're dying in the hot desert."

"This desert is haunted," explained Zinnia as she sidled up to him. "It shows you your heart's desire in the form of a mirage. Don't trust it."

"I'm trying not to," said Dodie, "but it keeps leading me off the course."

"I saw my dad." Zinnia's voice sounded choked.

"Sorry. I saw Taj."

"That makes sense."

"How do we get through this?" Dodie noticed the arrow below him again.

"We have to fly together. We have to keep each other from following the mirages we see."

"Two are better than one," Dodie said knowingly. He reached over and grabbed the edge of her carpet.

"You keep your eyes ahead, and I'll keep my eyes on the compass," she said.

Several times Dodie felt her carpet tug in his hand, and realized he must have started to veer off course. Zinnia's eyes never left the compass so she could keep them on course and keep herself from being tempted by a mirage.

The sky started to lighten, much to their relief. It was hard work flying close and keeping on course. A few times Dodie thought he saw Taj and Nadar in the distance, but he mustered enough self-control to ignore them. He had a hard time keeping that lump down in his throat. He was looking forward to the pit stop at dawn. He noticed that as the night wore off, so did the arrow and the sightings of his family. As the sun rose, bathing the Phantom Plains with golden light, the mirages faded completely.

"I think we're in the clear," he told Zinnia.

Zinnia looked up from her compass. "There's the pit stop!"

Ahead they could see a large red yurt posted at the foot of a mild mountain range. A stream trickled beside the yurt. Dodie and Zinnia landed and found they were the first ones to arrive.

"Maybe the others already stopped and moved on," Zinnia noted.

"I don't think so," said Dodie as he entered the yurt. "It doesn't look like any food's been eaten yet." He helped himself to the baskets of bread, apples, and raisins.

"Good, maybe we can get a head start before they arrive." Zinnia bit into an apple.

Just then Atallah strutted into the yurt, and pulled off his head mask.

"I thought you guys got bewitched out there," he smirked as he grabbed a piece of bread and stuffed it into his mouth. He chewed and swallowed. "Did you see your mommy out there, Rat Scat? Oh wait, she's dead."

"Shut up, Atallah." Dodie finished his apple and chucked the core to the ground. He threw a fistful of raisins into his mouth.

"How about you, Zin?" Atallah asked casually, swiping an apple. "Who'd you see? What's your story?"

Zinnia started to pass him.

Quicker than quick, Atallah reached out and whipped off her head mask.

Zinnia shrieked.

Dodie yelled.

Atallah gasped.

The three of them stood still, except for their eyes darting around at each other.

Slowly, a smile spread across Atallah's face. "You're good," he said to Zinnia. "You totally fooled me. I never would've guessed you were a girl." He grinned wider. "But that's the problem—you're a girl, and last I recall, girls can't race in the Grand Flyer."

"Too late," panted Zinnia. "I already am."

"Go right ahead," shrugged Atallah as he bit into his apple. "But if you win, you can't collect the prize. You'll immediately be disqualified. Unless . . ."

"Unless what?" Dodie spoke up.

"You knew all along, right?" Atallah pointed a finger at him. "Hmm, judges could rule that you were an accomplice. You should've reported her right away. You could be disqualified, too."

"Don't listen to him," said Zinnia. "That is *not* a rule."

"You said *unless*," Dodie pressed. "Unless what?"

"Well, there's no rule against racers sharing a carpet. You could ride with me, Zin," Atallah winked at her. "Then when I win we could share the prizes."

"No prize is worth that," Zinnia scowled. "Besides,

the rule states that to win the racer must come in first on his carpet. That would be you."

Dodie frowned. "There's another problem with Zinnia riding with you."

"Zinnia? Pretty name," Atallah chewed, the apple crunching in his mouth.

"You're not gonna win," Dodie continued with a glare. "If Zinnia wants to cross the finish line first, she should ride with me."

Atallah chortled. "Do whatever you want, *Zin*. Nothing changes the fact that you're a girl and you shouldn't be here." He tossed her head mask back to her and went outside.

Dodie was quiet, watching Zinnia as she stared at her feet.

"Well, that's that," she said finally.

"No, it's not," argued Dodie.

"What am I gonna do?" She turned to him, her eyes watering. "He'll rat me out as soon as we reach the Capital!"

"I'm curious," Dodie tried to sound delicate. "If you won, how were you planning to get away with it?"

"I wasn't going to reveal myself until after I made my wish. But now . . ."

"Listen, you must finish the race," Dodie told her, his voice growing stronger. "If you come in first and are disqualified, then the second place will win. That could be me. You'd help my odds."

"You know I want your brother to live . . . I just

really wanted my dad back." Zinnia sniffed and wiped her nose on her sleeve.

Dodie reached out and rested a hand on her shoulder. "After the race I'll help you look for him. We can put together a search party." He offered her a smile. "Finish the race. For yourself."

"Fine." She lifted her head a little higher and marched outside.

Dodie followed her and found the other racers just landing as Atallah prepared to leave. Dodie and Zinnia mounted their carpets.

"What are you doing?" asked Atallah.

"I'm finishing the race," said Zinnia as she pulled on her head mask.

"What for?" Atallah snorted. "You're as good as disqualified. You think I'm gonna keep your secret?" He shot off into the sky.

Dodie and Zinnia flew for the low mountain range as the sun climbed higher. As they entered the mountains, a cool breeze that smelled salty wafted past them.

"Is that the ocean I smell?" Dodie asked excitedly.

"Sure is!" Zinnia sounded excited too.

It took them only an hour to cross the mountains. On the other side the Siren Sea met them. White beaches stretched north, and turquoise-blue water sparkled east for as far as the eye could see. The thunderous sound of crashing waves grew stronger as they cleared the mountains, and sea gulls squealed. The sun felt warm, the salty breeze felt cool, and the sky was never bluer. A huddle of clouds rested on the horizon, but they appeared far away. The beach was smooth, but toward the north the coastline grew rocky.

"It's beautiful!" breathed Zinnia.

"I wish we could hang out here for a while," said Dodie.

Both had paused in midair to take in the scenery.

Atallah whizzed by them, hooting and whistling. "You snooze you lose, love birds!"

"On our way home we'll stop by here again, agreed?" Zinnia said, picking up speed.

"Agreed!" Dodie chased after her. Well, if he lost the race at least he'd have one thing to look forward to.

Chapter 13

Several times Dodie found his speed slackening because he was distracted by the ocean. The continuous motion of the waves crashing and receding mesmerized him. He felt small in this vast world where the sea stretched so far it eventually touched the sky. The cool breeze and salty spray rejuvenated him and filled him with a sense of empowerment, as if he could do anything he wanted . . . even win the Grand Flyer.

He and Zinnia stayed close together with Atallah a few yards ahead and Nye a few yards behind. Randi and Bae lagged in the rear. They flew across smooth beaches and soft surf for most of the morning. Dodie was enjoying the ride.

But then the sun rose higher in the sky and noon approached. Dodie had forgotten about the time until he started to feel a slight queasiness in his stomach. At first he wondered if he had eaten that food at the pit stop too fast. A sudden jolt of panic shot through him when he noticed, for the first time it seemed, how high up he was. Every little sway and bump over the wind started to feel stronger than it was. He had grown so accustomed to flying by now that it came as a shock when he realized he was feeling these sensations *because* he was flying. The potion was wearing off.

"Zinnia!" he called, his voice a little high. "The potion's wearing off."

Zinnia looked over at him, her dark eyes wide. "Can you hang on a few more miles? The last pit stop should be coming up."

"I'll try." Dodie gripped his carpet's braided loops tighter and took a deep breath of sea air.

He was thankful for the cool breeze and calming environment, for those would help him cope. He tried telling himself he wasn't afraid of flying, that he liked flying now, that he could do this on his own—but he didn't believe himself. It was like trying to convince himself he wasn't sick when his body told him otherwise.

Dodie lowered his altitude, thinking if he didn't have that far down to look he wouldn't be that afraid. It helped a little, but it also slowed him down, and he got splashed with water. He tried to keep *Phoenix* as steady as possible and avoided any turns. He kept his eyes locked on Zinnia in front of him.

But there was no ignoring the fear of flying that was rapidly suffocating him.

He noticed the coast changing from smooth beaches to rocky cliffs. He hoped the pit stop was soon, though once he landed he doubted there was any chance of getting back on his carpet.

Suddenly he perked up. What was that sound?

He looked around. Maybe he had imagined it, but he thought he heard . . . singing?

Maybe his fear was taking on new side effects, like hearing voices in his head. Not a good thing.

No! There it was again, and it was growing stronger.

Ahead of him, Atallah whooped and pointed down at a cluster of rocks jutting up from the waves. Dodie squinted against the bright reflections on the water, and saw three women perched on the rocks, their long wavy hair cascading around their shoulders. Their hair was black with blue and purple tints when the sunlight hit them, and their eyes were abnormally large and bright. Their skin was tan and shiny with salt water. Oddest of all, their legs were scaly and silvery, shimmering in the noon sun. Wait, they weren't legs at all.

"Mermaids!" squealed Zinnia. "Listen to them!"

The racers slowed down to admire the beautiful mermaids as they sang in high clear voices.

"We know the paths of the deep;
Rocked by the currents we sleep;
We hold secrets of the sea,
And have treasure to share with thee.
Our price is small to pay
Compared to the riches at bay;
Such wealth you cannot miss,
We ask for only one kiss."

One mermaid, her hair tied back with a strand of seaweed, reached down into the waves and brought up a fistful of gleaming white pearls. A second mermaid, with a starfish perched on her shoulder, held up brilliant red rubies in her palms. The third mermaid, who wore layers of shell necklaces, ran her hands through a pile of gold coins on her lap.

"All I have to do is kiss them and I get all that?" Bae gasped. "Deal!"

"Don't trust them!" warned Zinnia.

"Why not?" Bae swooped toward the mermaids.

"I've heard they can't be trusted."

"Yeah!" Dodie agreed, remembering his grandfather's warning. "Don't listen to their song or touch anything that shines."

"You're just superstitious." Bae glided to a halt beside the rock of mermaids. "I'm injured and have little chance of winning this race. If I can go home with some mermaid treasure I'll be happy."

Everyone pulled up to watch what would happen. The mermaids smiled, and it seemed like the very sunshine radiated from them. Bae stepped off his carpet and onto the rock. Each mermaid held out her treasure to him, and blinked her large luminous eyes. Bae grinned foolishly, clearly enamored by their beauty and attention to him. He turned to the mermaid who offered him handfuls of pearls.

"Just one kiss?" he asked her.

She nodded, and raised her face up to him. Bae

leaned down and closed his eyes. Their lips locked.

In a flash, the mermaid pulled Bae back into the water with her.

Everyone yelled, then waited for them to resurface. The mermaid's head broke up through the waves, and she dragged her body back up onto the rock. Bae was never seen again.

"Well, that's a heck of a way to go," Atallah muttered with a snicker, and took off.

The mermaids continued to sing in their lovely voices as they swished their silvery tails and held up treasure in their hands. The racers passed them and continued on their way.

Dodie had flown only a few yards when his stomach lurched and his heart hammered in his chest. It was no use; he couldn't avoid it any longer. He had to get his feet on solid ground. Without thinking, he landed on a solitary rock in the surf.

Phoenix rolled up beside him. Dodie sat gripping the rock, panting heavily. The cool spray from the waves felt good. The other racers, including Zinnia, continued on their way, unaware of him. Dodie didn't care. He didn't care about ever flying again. He couldn't think past his fear. All he cared about was staying on that rock . . . forever. He heard a splash, and looked around. A mermaid wearing a headdress made of white shells pulled herself out of the water and onto the rock.

Dodie crawled back to the edge of the rock. "Go away! Scram!" He shooed her with his hand.

The mermaid cocked her head to one side and stared at him without blinking her large eyes. Dodie had thought Zinnia had the prettiest eyes he'd ever seen, but they did not compare to the mermaid's. Her eyes were the color of the sea, and seemed to be brimming with a profound secret. Dodie didn't move a muscle as he watched her, and as he waited to see what she would do, he resolved not to kiss her.

He wondered if she would attack him. He was trapped there on that rock, for there was no way he could bring himself to mount his carpet and fly away. And he didn't know how to swim. He wondered how long it would take her to drown him. She opened her mouth, but Dodie cut her off before she could start singing.

"I don't want any treasure! I won't kiss you, so go away!"

Slowly the mermaid reached out her hand. Dodie stiffened. He clenched his fists, ready to fight her off if she tried to pull him into the water. She gently touched his arm. He held his breath.

"The sea has whispered words to me," she said in a high airy voice. "Powerful words about you."

"About *me*?" Dodie licked his lips. He noticed a large gold pendant engraved with a star hanging from the mermaid's neck. "Are you a Seer?"

The mermaid nodded. "*You will triumph over both soul and body and have a change of heart. At journey's end you will be victorious and find more than you seek.*"

Dodie stared at her, stunned. "N-no, that's my brother—not me. How did you . . . ?"

"You are marked with the flame of good fortune." The mermaid stared at his chest where his good luck charm was hidden beneath his tunic. "Claim your prophecy."

"Can't be me. I can't finish this race." Dodie felt his heart growing heavy by the minute as he realized the truth in his words. "I can't do it," he whispered. "I can't save Taj."

"The sea does not lie," the mermaid said, her voice hardening slightly.

Dodie looked at her. "But how?"

"Follow your heart." The mermaid reached up and pressed her palm against his chest.

He expected her hand to feel cold and clammy, but when she touched him warmth spread through him. Even when she dropped her hand, his heart still burned. He realized it was the good luck charm burning against his skin, and his heart blazed with courage. With a parting nod, she slipped off the rock and into the water. She disappeared below the surface.

Dodie sat on the rock, staring out at the horizon. He rubbed his chest where the clay flame rested, for he still felt warm.

Could it be true? Could the prophecy really be about him and not Taj? Come to think of it, the Seer never said Taj's name, and her eyes were masked so he couldn't tell who she had been looking at when she made the prophecy. Maybe she had declared those words over Dodie. If so, that changed everything. That meant he was destined to be here. That meant nothing could stop him from winning the Grand Flyer and saving Taj.

Not even his fear of flying.

Dodie stood up, his legs shaking.

"Phoenix," he whispered.

His carpet opened. He stared at her brilliant red, orange, blue, and gold colors blazing in a fiery design. *Phoenix* had believed in him from the beginning. Somehow he and his grandfather's racer rug had a magical connection that he couldn't ignore.

Maybe he wasn't a fraud. If the prophecy was about him, that proved he wasn't a fraud. A fear he had not realized he'd been harboring melted away—not the fear of flying, but the fear of not being good enough, the fear of being himself. Something changed inside him.

He was a Rue, and he was a racer.

And he wanted to fly.

Slowly, he placed one knee on the carpet. It felt sturdy. He brought his other knee up. When he gripped the braided loops, they felt familiar and right. He looked north where he needed to catch up to the other racers.

"Let's do this!" Dodie crouched low and held on tightly.

Phoenix shot off.

He laughed.

He had never felt so free in his life. He was free of his queasy stomach, his crossed eyes, his hammering heart, his sweaty palms.

He was free of his fear.

And for the first time ever, he truly enjoyed the flight. Even though the potion had numbed his fear, it had also numbed his senses from fully experiencing flying. Now he felt every thrill, and it exhilarated him. He truly felt himself.

"Faster!" he commanded *Phoenix*.

She responded with a burst of speed that defied all carpet manners. Dodie's hands tingled as he gripped her loops, and he could feel the magic between them. Soon he caught up to Zinnia, who was not far behind Atallah, Nye, and Randi.

"Hey!" Zinnia shouted excitedly. "What happened to you?"

"Something great."

They soon found the last pit stop posted atop a cliff over the ocean. Everyone stopped and hurriedly scarfed down food and water in the red yurt. No one said much as they ate their food and took in the spectacular view of the ocean from atop the high cliff. The clouds that had seemed so far away were billowing closer. They were dark, bringing with them a change in the wind. A storm was coming.

"Well, this is it," Randi said. "May the best man win."

They were all standing on the edge of the cliff, making last minute adjustments to their head masks, waist pouches, and carpets.

"Thanks," said Nye in a deep voice. "Though that man won't be you."

He shoved Randi over the cliff's edge.

Everyone shrieked. Randi screamed as he fell down, then was silent as he hit the jagged rocks below. The waves swallowed him up.

"What did you do?!" yelled Dodie, backing away from the edge.

Nye rounded on them. "Taking out the competition." He held up a dagger, its silver blade flashing in the sunlight.

"Whoa, calm down!" Atallah ordered, holding up his hands in defense. "Let's get back to the race." He hopped on *Sky Cleaver* and took off.

"Zinnia, go!" Dodie yelled, opening *Phoenix.*

Zinnia scrambled onto *Amethyst* and flew up.

"I will stop at nothing to win," growled Nye as he mounted his carpet, dagger still in hand.

"This is not the way to win." Dodie shot off, coaxing as much speed as he could from *Phoenix.* Up ahead he could see Atallah and Zinnia while behind him he heard Nye.

Nye caught up alongside him and swiped at Dodie with his dagger.

Dodie dodged to the left.

Nye closed in again and took another jab.

"Back off!" cried Dodie.

Nye lunged at him.

Dodie grabbed Nye's wrist. Nye pulled Dodie

toward him. Dodie let got, almost toppling off his carpet.

"Ouch!" Dodie felt his hand sting where Nye's dagger nicked him. Dodie didn't know what do, for Nye was not backing down.

Carefully Nye started to stand up to gain the higher ground. He gripped his dagger, and his eyes grew cold. He wanted blood.

Dodie swallowed.

Nye sliced the air at Dodie.

Dodie felt *Phoenix* lift and tilt so her underside faced Nye.

Suddenly sparks flew and Nye howled. His whole body shuttered and jolted and lit up as if lightning had struck him. Then with a blood-curdling scream, Nye fell off his carpet and plummeted to the rocks below.

Dodie looked back in time to see his body get washed away by the waves, along with his black and red carpet.

"You saved my life again," he muttered to *Phoenix*. "I'm not sure how, but you did. That was some magic."

Chapter 14

One in twenty-five.

Those had been the odds of Dodie winning when he had first taken off almost three days ago.

One in three.

Those were the odds now as he caught up to Zinnia and Atallah.

And really he had a fifty-fifty chance of saving Taj because as long as Atallah came in third place he would get a wish either by winning or by coming in second to Zinnia by default. Dodie was feeling the most confident he had during the Grand Flyer so far. Being free of his fear contributed to that confidence as well.

"Where's Nye?" asked Zinnia as he sidled up to her.

"He fell off his carpet." Dodie told her what had happened when Nye's blade had struck *Phoenix*.

"That's some magic carpet you have there," she said. "We gotta make sure Atallah comes in third."

Dodie skimmed a large rock jutting up from the waves. "I'm not gonna play dirty though."

"Technically there's no playing dirty in this race," said Zinnia. "There's no rule that—"

"That's not who I am!" Dodie cut her off. "I'm not Nye or Atallah."

"No, you're not, and that's why we're friends." Zinnia flew closer to him and reached out for his hand.

Dodie felt his heartbeat quicken, and his mouth dry up. He held very still, afraid any movement would make her hand slip off his.

"What are you guys conspiring back here?" Atallah suddenly appeared on Zinnia's other side.

Dodie glowered at him. "How to make sure you come in last."

"Ha! There's no chance I'm coming in last to a rat catcher who can't fly and a *girl*. The genie might as well grant me my wish right now. It's as good as mine, losers!" Atallah drifted closer to Zinnia. "You ready to give the victor a kiss? That's what the damsel always does."

"You wish! And I'm not a damsel—I'm a racer!"

"Believe what you want, *Zin*, but all wishes come true."

"Come on, Zinnia, ignore him," said Dodie, veering away from Atallah. "He's not gonna win that wish, right?"

"Right!"

"Wrong!" Atallah knocked into Dodie.

"Lay off!" Dodie shouted as he swerved away.

The sky was darkening with storm clouds, the wind

was picking up, and the waves were swelling. Somewhere across the ocean, thunder made an announcement. The three racers gripped their loops and braced themselves as they flew into the storm. They found themselves trapped between the tall rocky cliffs of the shoreline and the pounding waves growing in height with every swell. They tried to fly higher above the cliffs but the wind was too strong, not to mention the Boundary. They slowed down to dodge the waves ramming the cliff.

"This is gonna be tricky to get through!" Dodie shouted above the storm.

"We gotta stick together!" yelled Zinnia. "That way if one of us falls, we'll be there to catch him."

"Ha!" Atallah hollered. "I'm not going back for either of you if you fall!"

"I wasn't talking to you!" screamed Zinnia. She pulled up sharply, just missing a wave as it crashed against the cliff.

Dodie bumped into her from behind and caught spray from the wave. He felt Atallah nudge him in the back, and it made him nervous. He didn't like being so close to Atallah; no telling what he might do. At least the storm was keeping all three of them completely focused. For Dodie, it took every ounce of control and concentration to keep *Phoenix* from being carried off by the wind or drowned by the waves. He also had to watch the swells and predict when they would peak and crash, and time his pace accordingly. As the storm intensified, the waves came faster and harder until there was barely a break between them to get through.

Dodie was soaked. He stripped off his head mask and flung it away. He was feeling queasy, but he couldn't spare any attention on that. Squinting his eyes against the pelting rain, he ignored how cold he was. He heard a muffled yelp behind him, and turned to look. Somehow he had gotten ahead of Zinnia. They were separated by a few yards of towering waves. He didn't see Atallah anywhere, and he whipped his head around, searching for the blue-eyed boy, for he would feel better knowing where he was.

"Whoa!" He felt *Phoenix* pull up beneath him just as a wave roared in front of them. He couldn't afford to look for Atallah, or even keep an eye on Zinnia. He had to watch his path.

Phoenix was sopping wet, and Dodie wondered how she was still able to stay aloft. They inched their way up the coast. With the sun blocked, Dodie had no idea what time it was, and hoped the Capital wasn't too far off. He couldn't see more than a few yards ahead of him.

For the first time in the last three days, Dodie desperately wished he was anywhere but there at the moment. He was wet, cold, achy, and lost. He couldn't think of being any more miserable—well, throwing up would be slightly worse. His stomach lurched and he thought of something else.

He thought of Taj. He thought of his life without

Taj, and this made his throat tighten. He remembered his last view of Taj passed out on his cot, looking as pale as death. Taj didn't belong on that cot; he belonged on his racer rug. Dodie's face was streaming with water, so he couldn't tell if he was crying. He stopped thinking such bleak thoughts and instead thought about a happier future with his brother. Now that Dodie was no longer afraid of flying, he could join Taj in racing practice, and get one-on-one flying instructions from him. He smiled.

Next, he thought of Zinnia and her desperation to find her father that had driven her to chop off her hair and fearlessly compete against boys. He thought of the mermaid who had recited the prophecy about him, and this made his heart warm. He thought—

Wait!

Far ahead in the distance, the sun was leaking through the clouds, and Dodie caught a brief glimpse of tall steeples and turrets.

The Capital.

He wasn't too far now. A few more miles, a few more waves to dodge, and he would be in the clear. He could hardly believe it, and yet he wasn't too surprised that he had almost made it. By the looks of it, he would get there first.

He would win.

"You're still here, huh?" Atallah hollered over at him.

Dodie started, shocked to find Atallah suddenly

next to him. "Where've you been?"

Atallah, unmasked, grinned. "It'll take more than a storm to get rid of me."

"Guess it's you and me, neck in neck to the end," shouted Dodie, watching Atallah out of the corner of his eye as he skimmed a wave.

"No way!" Atallah dove for him.

Dodie expected this move, and was ready for it. He shot out a hand to block Atallah, and knocked him in the chest.

Atallah swung back, connecting with Dodie's shoulder. He kicked Dodie in the ribs.

Dodie winced, trying his best to stay on his carpet and dodge the pounding waves. Atallah came at him again. Dodie jabbed, but missed and almost fell off *Phoenix*.

Atallah grabbed Dodie's wrist and pulled. Dodie kicked Atallah off.

A large wave loomed for them. Dodie darted up to miss it. Suddenly he felt a great weight pull his carpet. He thought a wave had gotten him, but when he looked over his shoulder, he saw Atallah hanging off the edge of *Phoenix*. *Sky Cleaver* was being drowned by the sea.

"Help me!" screamed Atallah.

Dodie growled in frustration. It would be so easy to let Atallah fall. His life would be better for it, but Dodie couldn't do it, so he reached out a hand to help Atallah up.

Atallah scrambled onto *Phoenix*.

F.C. Shaw

"Thanks," Atallah panted. "for helping me up. And for your rug."

"For my—?"

Atallah shoved Dodie off the carpet.

Dodie yelled as he tumbled through the air. A wave caught his feet, and slammed him against the cliff. He was sure every bone in his body was broken.

But he managed to cling to the rocks.

Crash!

A wave slammed him. He went under. He couldn't see, he couldn't breathe. He felt an immense pull as the wave receded, but he held onto the rocks with every last bit of strength. He couldn't be swept into the churning water or he would surely be done for.

His numb legs and arms still worked, so he started climbing higher to escape the waves.

Crash!

He held his breath and closed his eyes this time. He tasted blood in his mouth. The receding wave sucked him back, but Dodie held on. His fingers trembled and warm blood streamed from his palms where the rocks cut into him. He climbed higher.

He cried out. His entire body was racked with pain.

He heard another wave roaring toward him, wanting to devour him.

"Do your worst!" he cried, gritting his teeth with determination.

Crash!

The wave answered him with such force that Dodie

160

nearly blacked out.

When the wave retreated, Dodie was still clinging to the rocks. He climbed again, but slipped.

He hung there, barely breathing, dreading the next bombardment. He wasn't sure how much longer he could hold on. He was exhausted, his whole body throbbed with pain. The idea of being carried away by the sea was now appealing. Maybe drowning wasn't so dreadful. Maybe—

"Dodie! Hold on!"

He looked up.

Crash!

Another wave smashed him. He couldn't hear or see anything. His head broke through as the wave fell back. He gulped air.

He looked up and saw Zinnia atop the cliff, reaching her hands down to him. He was nearly at the top. He reached up and gripped her hand. Their hands slipped apart, for his was wet with water and blood.

"Come *on!*" shouted Zinnia, her unmasked face fearful. "Climb higher!"

Dodie climbed up and clenched her hand. She grabbed his other wrist with her other hand and pulled. Dodie used his feet to help. He dragged himself to the top as a wave crashed just below him, spraying him one last time.

Dodie rolled over on his back, and lay there panting, feeling the soft rain trickle over him. Next he saw Zinnia's face above his.

"That was close," she panted in between rapid breathing. She leaned down and pressed her face against his.

Dodie closed his eyes and felt her cold cheek.

"Are you okay?" she whispered in his ear.

"Dunno."

She sat up and gripped his arms. "Try sitting up."

Slowly, and with great effort not to whimper, Dodie sat up and surveyed his body. Patches of blood seeped through his tunic in random spots on his torso and legs. His palms were scraped nearly raw. He could still move his arms and legs, but a deep jabbing pain told him he had broken a rib or two.

"Where's Atallah?" asked Zinnia, fetching her jar of healing ointment. She started dabbing Dodie's face with it.

"Gone. He shoved me off and left. He's probably already at the Capital." Dodie took a deep breath as the ointment relieved the pain on his face.

"The going is slow, he's probably not there yet," said Zinnia, rubbing the ointment on Dodie's palms. "Still, it'll be hard catching up to him."

"I was so close," Dodie said, his voice croaky. "Taj will die. I can't—"

"Don't say that!"

"It's true!" he yelled in her face. "All this was for nothing!"

Zinnia opened her mouth, but nothing came out. A few drops trickled down her cheeks, and Dodie couldn't tell if they were raindrops or teardrops. Either way, her face was marked with sincere grief, and he loved her for it.

Without another thought, he grabbed her and hugged her. She did not pull away, but tightened her arms around him, which hurt like crazy, but he didn't care. They sat there on the cliff, holding each other, as the sea settled down and the clouds broke apart.

Finally he released her. As bad as their situation was, Dodie did not want to move on from this moment with her. If nothing else, it delayed his having to face defeat . . . and the death of his brother.

"Where's *Phoenix*?" asked Zinnia, looking around the cliff top.

"Atallah stole her," mumbled Dodie.

Zinnia snapped her eyes back to him. "He *stole* her? You're sure?"

Dodie felt slightly annoyed. "Yes! He lost his carpet, so I pulled him onto mine. He shoved me off and sped away on *Phoenix*."

Zinnia shot to her feet, a new fire in her eyes. "Get up. Let's go."

"What's the point?"

Zinnia smiled, that fire intensifying. "This race is far from over."

Dodie furrowed his brow, then his face broke into a wide grin as he caught on to what she was thinking. "You're right! This race is definitely *not* over yet!"

Chapter 15

"Zinnia, what are you doing?" demanded Dodie as he watched her carry her rolled-up carpet over to him.

She dropped her racer rug at his feet. "I'm giving *Amethyst* to you."

"You don't need to do that." Dodie rolled his eyes. "I'm not leaving you here."

"No, we'll both ride her to the Capital." Zinnia pulled him to his feet.

Dodie yelped in pain, but was able to stand. He hugged his throbbing side and had to take shallow breaths.

"But it's crucial that you own *Amethyst*." Zinnia gave her rug a nudge with her toe. "I'm *giving* her to you." She grabbed Dodie's hand and pressed it on top of the carpet. "I hereby give you *Amethyst*, Dodie Rue."

Dodie held his hand over the rolled up carpet. "*Amethyst*," he muttered.

The racer rug unrolled itself, her fuchsia and silver swirls looking more beautiful than ever.

Zinnia smiled with satisfaction. "Let's go." She mounted the carpet, leaving room for Dodie to sit in the front.

Dodie climbed onto *Amethyst* and crouched down with a wince. "We might not be able to outrun Atallah, but we can outsmart him," he said slyly.

Dodie took them up. He found *Amethyst* to be very speedy and easy to guide, but not nearly as agile as *Phoenix*. He hoped he could reclaim his grandfather's racer rug, for losing *Phoenix* would only add to the shame of losing the Grand Flyer.

They sped toward the Capital that was in plain view ahead. Just outside the front gates to the city was the finish line. Colorful banners flapped in the wind, torches lined the final runway, and masses of people cheered on either side of the torch-lined runway. A tall stand stood at the end of the runway where the judges presided.

"There's Atallah!" Dodie pointed. "He must've gotten slowed down by the storm."

About twenty yards ahead, Atallah zoomed on *Phoenix.* He was almost to the finish line.

Dodie tried to coax more speed out of *Amethyst,* but it was no use.

Atallah streaked down the runway amidst wild cheers from the crowds. He hovered beside the judges' stand and waved victoriously to the spectators.

Dodie and Zinnia sailed in next and received cheers as well, though they weren't as enthusiastic.

F.C. Shaw

Dodie scanned the crowds, hoping to see his family, but there were too many people to distinguish faces. Plus he figured everyone had stayed home with Taj.

The crowd hushed as the Magistrate of the Capital raised his hands to address them.

"Congratulations to all our contestants, and especially to these three who have completed the Grand Flyer!" boomed Magistrate Obenido.

The crowd cheered briefly before the Magistrate continued his speech.

"We have our clear champion here!" He gestured to Atallah who beamed. "Atallah Hadi from Turah!"

Atallah zipped over the crowd, and skimmed their heads and threaded on the city walls. The crowd went wild.

"Get closer to the Magistrate," Zinnia said behind Dodie.

Dodie glided up to the judges' stand.

"Please, sirs, there's been a mistake," said Zinnia.

The judges glared down at her.

The Magistrate looked appalled. "You're a girl! Females are forbidden to race in the Grand Flyer! Who are you?"

"That doesn't matter," said Zinnia, her voice finding strength. "What matters is that Dodie Rue is the rightful winner, not Atallah."

"How do you figure that?" demanded Magistrate Obenido. "Atallah clearly arrived first."

"No, sir!" continued Zinnia.

"Atallah won on a stolen carpet!" Dodie jumped in.

The judges murmured together. Magistrate Obenido eyed Dodie and Zinnia with new interest.

"He *stole* that carpet?" Obenido pointed a chubby finger at *Phoenix*.

By now, Atallah had noticed Dodie and Zinnia conversing with the judges, and he sped over to them.

"Poor loser, eh, Rat Scat?" he sniggered as he stood atop *Phoenix* with his arms crossed.

"That's my racer rug," said Dodie, glaring at Atallah. "You pushed me off and stole her."

"That's a lie!" Atallah snarled. "*Phoenix* is and always has been *my* carpet."

The judges huddled together for a minute, then Magistrate Obenido addressed them. "This is a serious charge, but we must test it. Atallah, dismount your carpet and ignite her again. You must prove she's yours."

"This is ridiculous!" Atallah screeched, throwing his hands up. "I shouldn't have to prove anything! I'm the Grand Flyer champion, and I won on *my* carpet."

"I'm sorry, we must be sure. That's the rule." Obenido's face hardened, and he gestured his hand to the ground. "If you please."

With a huff, Atallah swooped down to the ground, and jumped off *Phoenix*. Immediately the carpet rolled herself up. Atallah held a hand over her and said, "*Phoenix*."

The carpet remained rolled up at his feet. The crowd stirred.

"*Phoenix!*" Atallah gave the rug a kick.

But the carpet did not open or even budge.

Dodie landed next to him, held a hand over his racer rug, and said her name. *Phoenix* unfurled herself and dazzled the crowd with her flaming colors and gold shine.

Magistrate Obenido raised his voice and announced, "Atallah Hadi, you are hereby disqualified from the Grand Flyer for finishing on a stolen racer rug!"

"They can't win either!" screamed Atallah, pointing at Dodie and Zinnia. "She's a girl! And that carpet is hers, not his!"

"That's not true!" Zinnia yelled back.

She jumped off *Amethyst*, causing the carpet to roll up.

"This carpet belongs to me, too," said Dodie. He ignited *Amethyst*, causing the crowd to gasp.

"He can't own *two* carpets!" argued Atallah.

The Magistrate turned his back on the crowd to confer with his judges. The crowd was silent with suspense. Atallah glared at Dodie and Zinnia. Zinnia squeezed Dodie's hand. Dodie's heart pounded in his chest. Finally Magistrate Obenido turned to face the contestants and the crowd.

"There is no rule against a racer owning more than one rug," stated the Magistrate. "As long as a racer finishes the race on his own rug, he qualifies. Therefore, our Grand Flyer champion is Dodie Rue from Turah!"

The crowd erupted into deafening cheers. Atallah

roared. Zinnia threw her arms around Dodie's neck. Dodie felt an overwhelming relief flood his body. He had made it, and he was alive. The best part was his brother would live, and his family would be released from their debt.

Suddenly he felt Zinnia ripped from him. Atallah had yanked her back and thrown her to the ground. Next he tackled Dodie to the dirt. Dodie caught the flash of a knife. The crowd screamed, and Zinnia cried out. Dodie felt a cold blade against his throat.

A troop of guards fell upon Atallah and pulled him off Dodie. They shackled his hands behind his back and dragged him through the city gates.

"I deserve to win!" roared Atallah as he was dragged away. "You're *nothing*! I was the better racer!"

The guards hustled Atallah into the Capital, and the crowd drowned out his cries.

"Dodie Rue!" Magistrate Obenido called from his stand. "Your wish shall be granted tomorrow at dawn, and your treasure will be delivered to you next week. Congratulations to our rightful winner of this year's Grand Flyer—Dodie Rue!"

As the crowd cheered, Dodie turned to Zinnia. He pressed her hand on the rolled up *Amethyst*.

"I hereby give you *Amethyst*, Zinnia," he told her. "She's yours again."

Zinnia smiled, but behind her smile Dodie could see sadness in her eyes, and he knew why. Even though she never had a chance to win the wish once she was exposed as a girl, he knew it was still painful for her to lose the hope of seeing her father again.

Dodie and Zinnia were ushered into the city where they were honored with a great banquet of celebration. Dodie's victory was dispatched to all five competing towns through a network of five Wishing Wells. He would have loved to see his family's reaction to the news.

He and Zinnia spent the night in the Magistrate's mansion. Their rooms were across the hall from each other. A hot bath with flower-scented oils was drawn in Dodie's room. As soon as he sank into the water, his body relaxed, and he nearly fell asleep soaking in it. When the water cooled, he got out and dressed in a soft linen robe laid out for him. He attacked the platter of meats, cheese, bread, and fruit, and downed several large goblets of water. He felt so much better. The Magistrate's personal physician attended to Dodie's multiple wounds and bandaged his torso, assuring Dodie his fractured ribs would heal with time. He drank a soothing herbal tea that put him into a deep, restful sleep. He didn't even dream.

Dodie awoke just before dawn feeling completely rested. He lay on the over-sized pillows for a few minutes thinking about the race, about meeting the genie, and about Zinnia. He would make good on his promise to help search for her father, though he had no idea where to start looking for someone who was supposedly *swallowed* up by the desert, whatever that meant. Dodie sat up with a sudden thought. He wondered . . .

Two servants entered his room, and brought a royal blue tunic for him to wear and a plate of fruit and yogurt. When they left, Dodie got dressed and ate his breakfast. He was about to leave the room when he heard voices out in the hallway. He paused to listen, and recognized Magistrate Obenido and Zinnia speaking in low tones.

"I had no idea who you were at first," Obenido was saying. "You have great courage, but it doesn't change the rules."

"I know, sir. I just want my father back," said Zinnia.

The Magistrate heaved a sigh. "As do I."

"But you've given up on him," answered Zinnia, her voice hardening.

"We searched far and wide for him," said Obenido.

"He's not dead," Zinnia murmured.

"I would like to believe that," muttered Obenido. "After all, he wasn't called the Great for nothing. We've lost a brilliant alchemist, and you a wonderful father."

Dodie opened the door and met Obenido and Zinnia in the hallway.

She looked rested and as beautiful as ever with her short hair washed and her skin clean. She wore deep purple robes and gold bangles, and smelled like jasmine. She greeted him with a smile.

"I'm allowed to go with you to the genie—if that's okay," she added hastily.

"Of course you're coming with me." Dodie couldn't take his eyes off her. "You should've won. I couldn't have—"

"I don't wanna hear it," she cut him off. "You couldn't let your brother die."

"But your father—"

"I'll find him some other way." She didn't sound too confident.

"We both will," added Obenido. "Now, Dodie, you know the genie's rules on wishes? Good. And you've thought long and hard about your wish? Good."

Dodie turned to Zinnia and started to ask her the name of her father, but Obenido continued.

"Once we set foot on the mount, we must observe an attitude of silence in reverence to the genie. Do *not* utter a word inside the shrine except for your wish. Be sure to word it very specifically. Follow me."

Silently they walked out into the open courtyard, then headed out of the Magistrate's house. Dodie and Zinnia followed Obenido through the stirring streets and up a hill that overlooked the city. Fresh sunshine promised a beautiful spring day. At the top of the hill was a golden shrine that hurt their eyes in the morning light. They gathered just outside the shrine's door. Obenido fished out a large skeleton key strung on a leather chord around his thick neck, and unlocked the shrine door.

Dodie stepped inside, Zinnia right behind him. The shrine was still cold from the night, and weak light filtered through a single hole in the roof. A shaft of light spotlighted a pedestal in the center of the room, upon which rested a golden lamp.

Dodie edged closer to the lamp, feeling a sense of awe. The golden lamp was polished—except for a patch on its side that had been rubbed dull countless times by countless men through the ages. Slowly Dodie reached his hand out and rubbed the worn spot on the lamp's side.

A wisp of powder-blue smoke curled up from the lamp. As it rose, the vapor expanded and filled the shrine, causing Dodie and Zinnia to take a few steps back from the lamp. The form of a man from the waist up materialized in the smoke. He was nearly transparent, but the powder-blue smoke helped define him. He wore no tunic, only cuffs on his wrists and a hoop in his ear. His pointy face bore no expression, and he seemed not to notice Dodie and Zinnia. Instead he gazed vacantly at the ceiling.

"Your wish is my command," the genie said in a hollow monotone voice.

Dodie swallowed.

Zinnia nudged him.

Dodie took a deep breath. "Genie," he began.

The genie nodded his head.

"I wish for Zinnia's father to return to her right here, right now."

Chapter 16

The genie bowed. "Your wish is granted."

"*What?!*" shrieked Zinnia. "No! He wishes for his brother's life to be saved!"

The genie dissolved away and the powder-blue smoke sucked back into the lamp.

Zinnia spun around to face Dodie. "What did you do?"

Dodie took a deep breath. "You heard me."

"Why? What about Taj? I don't understand." Zinnia was openly crying.

Dodie couldn't tell if she was angry, sad, or happy.

"Why did you wish for my father?" she choked in between sobs. "Why would you . . . do that . . . for me? What . . . about your . . . brother?" She could barely speak through her crying.

Dodie tried not to watch her cry. "Because this way we both get what we want."

"How?" she sniffed.

"Your father can save my brother."

Zinnia stared at him. "What do you mean?"

"You told me your dad was a great alchemist. I overheard the Magistrate call him *the Great*."

Zinnia wiped her face. "Yes, that's true. But—"

There was a loud pounding on the shrine's door outside, and Dodie hurried to open it.

"He appeared out of thin air!" Magistrate Obenido exclaimed, clutching his heart in shock. "I assume you wished for his appearance?"

"Zinnia!"

"Father!"

A man with unkempt hair and beard and wearing tattered clothes threw his arms around Zinnia. The two buried their faces in each other's necks and sobbed together. Dodie stood off to the side, watching the reunion with a mixture of happiness and awkwardness. To his astonishment, he realized this was the man from his dream, the man who had conjured a cobra from the green liquid. When they parted, they turned to him.

"Thank you, my boy, thank you!" Zinnia's father exclaimed, stretching his arm out to Dodie and embracing him.

"Dad, this is Dodie Rue," said Zinnia. "Dodie, this is my father—"

"Zalla the Great!" Dodie finished breathlessly. "The most powerful alchemist of our time."

Zalla smiled, the creases around his eyes deepening. "If there is any way I can repay you, if there is anything I can do—"

"Yes, sir!" Dodie said immediately. "You can save my brother. He's been poisoned by Devil's Kiss, and the alchemist in town says there's no antidote."

"There is an antidote, but it requires very complicated alchemy," said Zalla, scratching his bearded chin. "But I know how to make it. When was he poisoned?"

It seemed ages ago that Dodie had attended the Magistrate's Banquet, watched his brother succumb to the poison, and entered the Grand Flyer.

"About five days ago, sir."

Zalla's face clouded. "That doesn't leave us much time. If not treated by the seventh day, the poison will induce death."

"Can we make it back in time?" asked Zinnia as she clung to her father's arm. "Back to Dodie's village?"

"Turah," Dodie clarified.

Zalla gaped in shock. "Turah, did you say? That's where I've been held captive!"

"*What?!*" Zinnia shrieked for the second time that morning. "By whom?"

"I'll tell you all about it along the way." Zalla started down the hill. "We must leave immediately if we are to make it back in time to save your brother, Dodie. We will make no stops."

"It is good to have you back," Magistrate Obenido said, shaking Zalla's hand. "What do you need from me?"

When they told the Magistrate of their dire situation, Obenido was very helpful in quickly packing food and water for them to take. He also generously gave them a small sprinkling of stardust to give them a head start. They agreed *Phoenix* should take the lead, and tied *Amethyst* to her back tassels so they wouldn't get separated. This way they could also take turns sleeping, for they couldn't afford to stop for a minute. Within the hour, they left the Capital. *Phoenix* drank up the stardust and rocketed off with *Amethyst* in tow.

The day was bright and clear, the ocean and sky a matching hue of brilliant blue-green. They zoomed down the coast of the Siren Sea so fast that they couldn't take in any details or even hear the waves. The stardust lasted a good thirty minutes, in which they covered hundreds of miles, and as they eased into a more moderate speed, they were able to enjoy the scenery.

Zalla knew a more direct route that took them down the coast for most of the journey, then cut across the mountains straight to Turah. Dodie was glad they wouldn't have to navigate Quillian's Pass, evade the ghoul, or dodge dragons again. Around midday, Zinnia passed out bread and cheese. She and Dodie sat cross-legged on *Amethyst* while Zalla guided *Phoenix*. As they ate their lunch, Zalla told them his story.

"I was making my journey to the Capital along my usual route, which took me past Turah. I don't usually stop in villages, because when people find out who I am, they come with all manner of requests for potions and miracles. But I discovered that I had forgotten to bring along a healing herb that helps me with the headaches I sometimes get from too much sun. I had a long way to go to the Capital, and knew I would need that herb. I had heard there was an aspiring alchemist in Turah, so I covered myself up and went looking for him. I figured he'd have the herb I needed, for it's a very common headache remedy. I found the alchemist in question, and he had the herb I needed."

"That was Raz," said Dodie.

"Yes, Raz," Zalla said darkly. "At first he had no idea who I was, and I wasn't about to tell him, but in the back of his shop there was a sudden explosion caused by his nephew experimenting with elements in an unsafe manner. Raz apologized, admitted to being an amateur, and confided that he had come across a deadly element with which he had no idea how to use or dispose of. The alchemist in me couldn't miss this opportunity to help and educate him. So I revealed who I was, and I gave Raz and his nephew a little lesson on how to handle the element. Biggest mistake of my life.

"At first Raz and his nephew peppered me with all sorts of alchemy questions, and showed me different experiments they had been working on—most of them had been performed on local palm trees and a few vermin. I was happy to help, but the hour was growing late. I needed to get back to my journey. I promised to stop by on my way home to give them further instructions.

"I was about to leave when suddenly I was knocked unconscious by a purple cloud, which was the potent sleeping drug Nightcall. When I awoke, I was locked in an underground cellar. Raz was desperate for more alchemy help, but could not afford formal lessons at the Capital because he was in deep debt already. He made me a deal: if I helped him with a few experiments, he would release me. He promised I could continue on my journey in three days. It seemed I had no choice, for I had no weapons on me, and he locked me up securely. I told him where I had left my camel packed with all my equipment—at an oasis just outside Turah—and he brought them to his shop. He took good care of my camel, but stole all my ingredients and books. After three days of helping him, I asked to be set free.

"But he needed more help. Days turned into weeks, and weeks into months. There was always something he needed help with, and he had the leverage. Once I realized he had no intention of letting me go, I stopped sharing my alchemy secrets and started giving him false information. Sadly, his nephew paid for it."

"What do you mean?" asked Dodie.

"Well, within a few weeks of staying there, I discovered that Raz's nephew was his personal punching bag for letting off steam when things didn't go his way. He started blaming Binni for the mistakes I was purposely making."

Dodie looked shocked. "You mean Raz beats Binni?"

Zalla nodded his head gravely. "I saw the evidence all over Binni right away, but didn't want to jump to any conclusions. After all, alchemy is a dangerous profession." Zalla pushed up his sleeves to reveal a plethora of scars on his arms. "But then I heard things, and a few times I saw Raz openly beat Binni. As much as I wanted to thwart Raz, I couldn't jeopardize Binni's safety. So I continued to help Raz, and Binni received fewer beatings. Most of my help involved simple healing potions and growth tonics, but I got worried that I may be causing more harm than good when one day Raz demanded Devil's Kiss."

Dodie and Zinnia gasped in unison.

"So Raz *did* have Devil's Kiss!" exclaimed Dodie. "He claimed he didn't carry it."

"It is one of the most deadly poisons, and it is manufactured in a very difficult way that only I know how to do," said Zalla.

"And only you know how to make the antidote, too," added Zinnia, glancing at Dodie.

"Correct. There is no other use for Devil's Kiss than to induce death, so I knew Raz was up to no good. By now it had been about four months of being held captive, and I was fed up. I refused to make Devil's Kiss for Raz. He threatened to torture me, and he did, but I still refused. Then he figured out Binni was my weakness. He threatened to torture Binni if I didn't comply. I knew he would, so I made Devil's Kiss." Zalla turned sorrowful eyes to Dodie. "I'm so sorry."

Dodie swallowed. "But you saved my best friend."

"I'm sure I did. Raz never told me who he used the

Devil's Kiss on."

"So did he poison my brother," asked Dodie, "or did he give it to someone else to use?"

"I'm willing to bet Raz used it himself, because when I questioned him about it, he shared that a prophecy had been made about him and his enemy," continued Zalla. "He needed to vanquish his enemy to fulfill the prophecy."

Dodie snorted. "What a lie! That prophecy said nothing about vanquishing an enemy. And besides, Taj was not an enemy! We've been family friends with Raz and Binni for years."

"I'm so sorry," Zalla shook his head. "I immediately brainstormed on a plan to escape. I had had enough, and as much as I didn't want Binni to suffer, I had a daughter to get home to. I was just working out details in my head of how I could get away when—*poof!* I found myself standing outside the genie's shrine!"

Dodie and Zinnia laughed. They spent the rest of the day sharing stories of the Grand Flyer. The sun set behind the rocky cliffs, the air cooled, and a light salty breeze followed them. They ate lamb strips and grapes for dinner. As night set in, Dodie felt his eyes grow heavy. Zalla assured them he was fine to fly for a while if they wanted to get some sleep. Dodie and Zinnia lay on their sides with their backs against each other. Dodie felt Zinnia's warmth next to him. For some time he watched the moonlit waves roll and topple, roll and topple.

He was so anxious to get home and see Taj. He hoped he had made the right choice in wishing for Zalla's return instead of Taj's life. In the moment it had seemed the right thing to do, and the smart thing to do so that both he and Zinnia could get what they wanted. He realized he would not have made that wish for anyone else, and wondered if his feelings for Zinnia were clouding his judgment. If Zalla was unable to heal Taj, Dodie would never forgive himself . . . and neither would his father and grandfather. Suddenly Dodie felt sick, but not from flying. He felt sick with worry. Eventually he fell asleep. He woke up some time later feeling a little cold. Zinnia was still asleep next to him.

"What time is it, do you think?" he asked Zalla in front of him.

Zalla did not turn around. "Around five. The sky is starting to lighten."

"Do you need a break? I can fly for a little bit."

Zalla shook his head, his wild hair ruffling in the breeze. "After sitting around locked up for months, it feels good to be flying. I'll sleep after breakfast. We should arrive in Turah before sunset."

Dodie lay his head back down and dozed off again. He felt Zinnia sit up, and when he opened his eyes the rising sun made him squint. He noticed the ocean was gone, for they had turned west into the desert. Dodie watched Zinnia dig through the pack of food, her cheeks aglow with rosy light.

"How'd you sleep?" she asked as she fished out

bread and cheese for breakfast.

"Good. I've never been able to sleep on a flying carpet before. It was comfy."

Zinnia tucked her short hair behind an ear. "We should let my dad get some sleep."

They paused in mid-air long enough for Zalla to switch places with Dodie and Zinnia. He curled up on *Amethyst* and soon fell asleep. Dodie flew *Phoenix* while Zinnia sat cross-legged behind him. They spent the morning recapping the Grand Flyer and its many perils. They ended in a fit of laughter as they remembered Atallah's shocked reaction to his defeat. They both agreed that he would probably return with a vengeance, and they'd have to be on their guard. Then they listed all the things they would wish for if they had unlimited wishes from the genie. Some of Zinnia's top wishes were for girls to be allowed to race in the Grand Flyer, for Atallah to be banished, and for the ability to fly without a carpet. Dodie came back with a wish for his grandfather to no longer be a cripple, for Atallah to be crippled instead (Zinnia laughed, then chided him for such a cruel wish), and for his family to be rich so his father wouldn't have to work so hard.

They ate the last of the food for lunch, saving some for Zalla when he woke up. For a few miles they rode in silence. Then abruptly Zinnia spoke, and when she did her voice sounded strained. Dodie did not turn to look at her, for he still felt awkward seeing her cry.

"I haven't thanked you yet," she said. "For returning

my father."

Dodie shrugged. "I know you were thinking it anyway."

"Would you have done that for another friend?"

Dodie didn't answer her.

"Like for your friend Binni?" she asked.

Dodie gave up. "No, Zinnia, I wouldn't have. I did it just for you." He kept his eyes ahead on the vast sand dunes. Quickly he added, "And I did it for Taj, obviously."

"Should I ask why?"

Dodie shrugged again. "If you want to."

"I don't think I need to," she said quietly. "Well, I would have done the same for you. For the same reason."

Dodie felt his face heat and his heart pound.

"Thank you," her voice suddenly sounded right in his ear.

He froze.

She lightly kissed his cheek.

He couldn't move, but he felt an overwhelming sensation bubbling up inside him.

Zinnia sat back down behind him.

For a few miles Dodie felt her kiss on his cheek. Once the bubbling inside him subsided, he could think more clearly about her kiss. When he was honest with himself, he had secretly yearned for a kiss. But it had caught him off-guard, and he had not reacted the way he had imagined he would. Now the moment was past.

Time slipped on so that now it was too late to respond to her kiss in any way. Even talking about it would be stupid. He felt like he had wasted the moment of a lifetime, and he hated himself.

But he didn't want Zinnia to think the kiss didn't matter to him, or that he didn't appreciate it, or worse that he hadn't felt it. She wasn't desperate enough to ask him about it either. He had to say something, or it would forever be the unfinished conversation between them that could potentially stain their friendship. He didn't want that!

He cleared his throat. "You're welcome," was all he could think of to say.

"What?"

With a sinking feeling he realized a good twenty minutes had now passed in silence since her kiss. She had probably moved on and was thinking of other things, namely what an idiot Dodie was.

Dodie tried again. "You're welcome . . . for saving your dad. And thanks . . . for the . . . kiss." He squeezed his eyes shut, wishing this awkward moment away.

Zinnia giggled softly behind him and rested a hand on his shoulder, which made everything feel okay again.

Later in the afternoon, Zalla woke up and ate the food they had saved for him. They paused again to switch places so he could drive *Phoenix* the rest of the way. Dodie and Zinnia sat side by side on *Amethyst*. As they started off again, Zinnia laid her head on Dodie's shoulder. He rested his cheek on the top of her head.

"Village ho!" Zalla hollered.

Dodie and Zinnia snapped their heads up, both of them blinking for they had started to doze. Ahead they could just make out the onion-shaped turrets and rusty-red rooftops of Turah. The sun was heavy in the west. They also noticed a long caravan of camels and merchants snaking past Turah. Not wanting any trouble from them, they skirted the town instead of flying through it, and soon spotted Rue's Rug Emporium. They swooped down and landed on the Rue's roof patio. Dodie jumped off the carpet and raced into the house, Zalla and Zinnia right behind him.

"Dad! Grandpapa! Taj!" Dodie shouted as he tore into their bedroom.

"Dodie! Is that you?" Nadar zipped over to him on his carpet, and engulfed him in a smothering bear hug. "Why are you back early? What happened? Did you not make your wish?"

"I'll tell you everything later," Dodie panted. "We have to save Taj first."

"Can't save him." Gamal's face fell.

Zalla stepped forward. "I can heal him. I am Zalla the alchemist."

"Zalla the Great?" Nadar stared at him in amazement. "You were presumed dead."

"What do you need?" Gamal cut in, rubbing his hands together. "To save Taj."

"I need a shallow bowl filled with water," Zalla began, rolling up his sleeves. He rattled off a list of random ingredients. "And lastly I will need a drop of blood from the one who poisoned him."

"We don't know who!" Gamal wailed.

Dodie turned to his father. "We do, Dad. It was Raz."

"No! He wouldn't—"

"It's true," Zalla spoke up. "We need his blood."

"I'll get it," Dodie decided.

"Should I go with you?" asked Zinnia.

Zalla shook his head. "I need you to help me with the antidote. It will take us about twenty minutes to prepare. Raz's blood is the last ingredient to add, and it must be added moments before Taj drinks it. By the looks of it, we don't have much time."

Dodie glanced over at his brother lying on his cot. Taj was white, his lips and eyelids were ashy, and his breathing came in wheezy gasps. He did not move.

"I'll get that blood," Dodie vowed, "or die trying."

Chapter 17

Dodie hopped on *Phoenix* and raced down the dusty street. The town wasn't too active, for most families had closed up shop and were gathering on their rooftops for twilight supper. Dodie was glad he wouldn't be noticed, for he couldn't be bothered by the villagers' inquiries about the Grand Flyer. When he arrived at the alchemist's shop, Dodie flew to the side alley. He hovered next to a window on the second floor.

"Binni!" he called.

Binni popped his head out the window. His face broke into a wide grin, his two front teeth bucking out like a rodent. "You're back already?! How'd it go? How are you flying without—"

"Binni, this is urgent!" Dodie cut him off. "Listen to me, I need a few drops of your uncle's blood."

Binni frowned. "What? That's about the weirdest thing you've ever asked for."

"I don't have time to explain," Dodie said impatiently. "Just get some for me, will you?"

"Fine."

"And don't tell him what it's for."

"What *is* it for?" Binni questioned, his eyes narrowing.

"It's for an antidote to save Taj," Dodie told him. "Now hurry!"

Binni disappeared inside. Dodie glided up and down the alley. The minutes dragged on. Dodie stopped to look in Binni's window. If Binni wasn't back in another minute Dodie would go in and look for him.

Another minute passed.

Dodie drifted in through the large window, and hopped off *Phoenix*, leaving her rolled up on the floor.

Binni walked in, and held up a tiny glass vial with a few scarlet drops. "I told him I needed it for my own potion-brewing and that—"

"Give it to me!" Dodie reached out for the vial.

"Binni!" a voice barked from the doorway.

Binni turned around. "Hey, Uncle, so—"

"You're back!" Raz looked at Dodie in surprise. "What do you need? Is it Taj?"

Dodie gulped. "Yeah, we have a chance to cure him."

Raz's gaze hardened. "Devil's Kiss has no antidote. He cannot be cured."

"Yes he can with a few drops of his poisoner's blood." Dodie locked eyes with the alchemist. "So we need yours."

Binni looked from his uncle to his friend. "What

are you talking about?"

"Go into the other room, Binni." Raz kept his cold eyes on Dodie.

"I don't understand, Uncle, what—"

"Go now!" shouted Raz. "And give me that vial."

Binni clenched his hand around the vial of blood. "Not until we figure out what this is all about. Dodie says he needs this to save Taj, so—"

"Taj cannot be saved!" Raz roared, wrenching the vial from his nephew. "I cannot allow it."

Dodie glared at him. "Why did you do it?"

"Because of the prophecy. He was to be champion and ruin me. He was to restore the great alchemist, and I would be ruined."

Dodie looked at him in confusion. "That's not what the prophecy said."

"That was *my* prophecy," Raz muttered. "I overheard the Seer's prophecy over Taj. Right after, I received a word from her that the Rue victor would restore Zalla the Great and the desert would swallow *me*."

Dodie reveled in this news. "So you made sure that neither prophecy would come to pass by murdering Taj."

Raz's eyes flashed. "I hated myself for doing it."

"You're a fraud!" Dodie snorted. "Your alchemy was stolen from Zalla, and to protect your dirty secret you were willing to kill an innocent person—my brother!"

"The Seer is never wrong," argued Raz.

"*You* were wrong though," said Dodie. "Those

prophecies weren't about Taj. They were about me. I'm the Rue victor."

His words struck Raz like a bolt of lightning. Before Raz could recover, Dodie lunged for him and grabbed his hand clutching the vial of blood.

"Take it easy!" Binni yelled.

Raz kicked Dodie off him. As Dodie tumbled to the floor, Raz bolted for the door.

Dodie got up and chased after him. Raz slammed the door in Dodie's face and locked it on the outside. Dodie pulled, pushed, kicked, and pounded on the door.

"This is crazy!" Binni hollered. "You need to calm down!"

Dodie spun around, and got right in Binni's face. "Back off! You knew your uncle was up to something—"

Binni threw his hands up in defense. "I swear I didn't! I would never betray my best friend!"

"Your uncle's been holding Zalla the Great!"

"Yeah, but my uncle told me Zalla was a wicked alchemist and if I said anything about him—" Binni stopped short, his face pale.

Dodie noticed a fresh bruise on Binni's temple. "He'd beat you."

Binni glanced nervously at the locked door. "I couldn't say anything," he whispered.

Dodie looked around Binni's room that was a complete mess of bowls, herbs, vials, stains, and other remnants of his many potion experiments. "How do you unlock the door?"

Binni frowned. "I can't unlock it from the inside. I've tried before."

Dodie realized being locked in his room was yet another abuse Binni regularly endured. "Come on!" He ignited *Phoenix*. He and Binni hopped aboard and flew out the window. They raced around to the front of the shop just in time to see Raz take off on his own flying carpet.

"There he goes!" Binni shouted behind Dodie.

Dodie chased after him. He felt a confidence bolster him, a confidence that came from having just survived one of the most brutal carpet races. A confidence from having conquered his own fears of flying. A confidence from owning his prophecies. He felt a surge of speed from *Phoenix*, as if she too shared his confidence.

Dodie came up behind Raz. "I won't let you get away!"

Raz threw something over his shoulder without turning around.

"Watch out!" warned Binni. "Snap crackers!"

Dodie swerved as an explosion boomed a few feet to their right, and destroyed the baker's awning. He stayed on Raz's tail as they flew out of the village. Raz turned around briefly to squirt a bright green liquid at Dodie.

Dodie managed to avoid most of it, but a few drops splattered his arm. The acid burned through his sleeve and into his skin. He gritted his teeth.

"Cut it out, Uncle!" yelled Binni.

Dodie had to stop Raz before they got too far across the desert. They neared the small oasis where Dodie had found his grandfather's emergency stash of stardust. Raz dove for the tree tops.

Whack!

A palm frond swiped through the air and knocked Raz off his carpet. He lost the vial.

Dodie did a nose dive; Binni gripped the back of his tunic. Dodie skimmed the sand, inches above the ground, and reached down to grab the vial that landed with a *clink*. He grabbed a fistful of sand with the vial, and urged *Phoenix* to climb up again.

Whack!

The palm branch hit Binni who did not know to duck. With a yelp, Binni fell off of *Phoenix.*

"Binni!" screamed Dodie. He swooped back around to pick up his friend, but stopped short.

Raz had mounted his carpet and caught Binni in mid-fall. He gained more altitude and hovered in place, glaring at Dodie who stopped a few yards away.

"Give me the vial!" hollered Raz. "And I'll give you Binni."

"Let Binni go!" yelled Dodie.

Binni struggled to get free, but Raz pinned his arms down and clenched a hand over the boy's mouth. "Give me the vial or Binni will die!" He whipped out a small bottle from his inner pocket. "Devils' Kiss!" He uncorked the bottle.

"No!" screamed Dodie. "Don't! He's your nephew!"

Raz brought the bottle to Binni's mouth, which he still covered with his hand. "Who will you save? Binni or your brother?"

Dodie licked his lips and felt his insides wiggle. His palms started sweating and he clenched the vial of blood harder. He was on the brink of vomiting. He felt the fear so keenly—the fear of failure again.

Click-click! Hiss!

A mound was moving beneath the sand, heading straight for the spot below Raz's hovering carpet. The mound rose.

"What's that?" screeched Raz as he watched the mound rise below him.

"Your failed alchemy!" said Dodie.

The sand fell away like water as a giant black mass materialized. First the tail with its razor sharp hook on the end reared up. Then came the plated body and the two front pincers the size of palm fronds.

Raz shrieked and started to fly away, but the scorpion's tail batted at him and snagged the carpet. Hooked on the tail's stinger, Raz could not escape. The scorpion yanked on the carpet.

Raz lost his grip on Binni. The boy fell off the carpet and landed in the sand a few yards from the scorpion.

Dodie swooped down. The scorpion crawled through the sand toward Binni, towing Raz and his carpet by the tail. Binni clambered to his feet and started running as fast as he could manage through the soft sand, his feet sinking with each step.

Click-click! The scorpion snapped his pinchers right behind Binni.

"Come on, *Phoenix*!" Dodie coaxed through gritted teeth.

With a burst of speed, *Phoenix* zoomed for Binni.

"Binni!" shouted Dodie. "Grab on! Fast!" He held out his hand as he raced toward his friend.

Binni reached up. Dodie grabbed Binni as *Phoenix* shot past the scorpion and up into the safety of the sky.

Hiss! The scorpion shook with rage.

Snap-crack! Raz threw down more snap crackers, but they fizzled out on the scorpion's armor.

The attack did not go unnoticed by the giant beast. It catapulted Raz off its tail.

Raz crashed into the sand. He shook his head, saw the scorpion coming, and scrambled to his feet. He started running.

"My uncle!" exclaimed Binni.

Dodie turned *Phoenix* around to go back for Raz.

Raz ran, his arms flailing in panic, his feet sinking in the sand. The scorpion closed in on him. Dodie raced for him.

Click-click! The pinchers caught its prey.

Raz screamed as the scorpion clamped him in its pinchers and burrowed down into the sand.

Binni covered his eyes, but Dodie watched as the scorpion and the alchemist disappeared into the earth.

"The desert swallowed him up," whispered Dodie.

He turned to Binni. "It's over. He's gone. You okay?"

Binni dropped his shaky hands from his eyes, and panted. "He was gonna kill me. He got what he deserved. But he was the only family I had."

Dodie put an arm around his friend. "No, he wasn't. You've got us."

Binni managed a small smile. "Thanks. Let's go save our brother then."

Dodie and Binni raced back to Turah, not stopping until they landed on the Rue's roof. They hurried into the house. Zalla was stirring a bowl of thick dark liquid, and Zinnia was sitting with Taj's head propped in her lap. Gamal and Nadar hovered nearby. The air smelled foul.

"I have it," panted Dodie, holding up the vial of blood. "It's not too late?"

Zalla took the vial from him and tapped the scarlet drops into the bowl he was mixing. "It's ready." He poured the potion into a smaller cup and brought it to Taj. "Open his mouth," he told Dodie.

Dodie moved his brother's lips apart.

Zalla carefully poured the scarlet potion down Taj's throat, just a little at a time. "Keep his head propped so he doesn't choke."

Zinnia tilted Taj's head up a little more. Zalla poured the last of the potion into Taj's mouth and stood back. Dodie closed his brother's mouth and stared anxiously at his pale face.

"Why's it not working?" Gamal hollered from the

corner.

"Give it a minute," whispered Zalla.

Gradually, the color came back to Taj's face.

"He's looking better!" exclaimed Binni.

Zinnia gently laid Taj's head back down and stood over by her father to watch.

Dodie knelt by his brother, waiting, barely breathing. "Come on," he whispered.

Taj's eyelids fluttered open, and he coughed. He looked at Dodie and gave a weak smile.

Dodie laid his head on his brother's chest, and heard a strong heart beat and steady breathing. Gamal and Nadar fell on Taj, not bothering to hold back tears. They helped Taj sit up a little on his bed.

"He will be weak until he gets nourishment," Zalla told them. "I'll prepare a tonic and a hearty broth for him."

He and Zinnia left the room to prepare the tonic and broth in the kitchen. Binni followed after them.

"What happened?" Taj asked in a hoarse voice.

"Your little brother just saved your life," said Nadar.

Taj looked at Dodie with a grin. "How'd you do that, Dodes?"

Dodie beamed. "I won the Grand Flyer."

Chapter 18

After Taj drank the tonic and broth that Zalla and Zinnia prepared for him, he felt strong enough to hear all about Dodie's adventures. Everyone gathered around Taj's bed to listen to Dodie and Zinnia's recount of the Grand Flyer. They were good story-tellers, painting rich descriptions of the scenery and building suspense at the dangerous moments of their journey. Nadar was thrilled that Dodie had heeded his map of secrets, and Zalla beamed at his daughter for her courage in racing against the boys. Taj never expressed any resentment over not racing, and instead swelled with pride over his little brother for doing so.

Their story ended on a sad note when they considered Binni who was now without his only relative; although knowing about Binni's abuse at home did not make them sorry that Raz was gone. While Binni was still feeling confused and hurt by his uncle, he was thrilled to sign on as Zalla's apprentice. Not only did Binni gain a kind master, but he also had his dreams fulfilled of learning alchemy.

At first Zalla considered taking Zinnia and Binni to live in the Capital where he held a prominent position on Magistrate Obenido's counsel. But Zinnia wouldn't hear of it. She wanted to live in Turah, and Dodie knew it was because of him. Zalla and Zinnia moved into Raz's shop with Binni. Zalla found all his books and tools and ingredients that Raz had stolen from him in addition to all Raz's equipment.

Magistrate Oxard hosted a celebration for Dodie at which Axel joined as the only other racer from Turah, for Atallah was still being held in the Capital. Axel had fully recovered from being poisoned and eagerly listened to Dodie tell him about the parts of the race he had missed.

Atallah was eventually released, but refused to return to Turah. His parents moved away and joined him at the Capital where the larger population made it easy to hide their shame. Dodie and Zinnia joked that her wish for his banishment had come true after all.

Before leaving Turah, Lord Hadi stopped by Rue's Rug Emporium. He did not hold his head nearly as high, and his large nose didn't look as prominent, for his whole demeanor had changed. He slapped a sheet of parchment on the counter. The paper was the written loan agreement both men had signed twelve years ago.

"We have a wager to settle," said Hadi in a low voice.

"We do," answered Gamal as he held out his half of

the winged amulet.

When both men placed their wings on the counter, the two wings united, glowed blue, then disappeared with a *poof.* Next the loan agreement magically ignited and burned into oblivion. Hadi frowned, and Gamal grinned.

Lord Hadi turned to leave when he spotted Dodie. "By all rights you shouldn't have won." His face was stoic, and for a moment Dodie wasn't sure what he would say or do next. Hadi grunted. "The universe makes strange calls. Who are we to argue with it?" He walked out of the emporium.

A few days later, race officials from the Capital arrived in Turah and delivered Dodie's winnings to Rue's Rug Emporium. They brought in a small heavy chest and handed over a gilded key. Dodie unlocked the chest to find it full of more gold coins than he had ever seen at one time before.

Taj whooped and ran his hands through the money. "I feel like a sultan!"

"Dad, this is for the shop. For us." Dodie pushed the chest down the counter to his father.

Gamal didn't reply, and when he looked up there were tears in his eyes. He didn't say anything to Dodie, but for the first time in a long while, he looked at his son without glassy eyes. And that was enough.

Nadar insisted that Dodie keep *Phoenix* as his own carpet now that he was a racer.

"We really took to each other," Dodie told his

grandfather as they sat on the roof stargazing.

"I figured you would," croaked Nadar.

"She did things that other carpets don't normally do."

Nadar nodded his balding head. "Magic."

"I love flying, Grandpapa," said Dodie. "And I feel like a Rue now."

"You've always been a Rue. Flying a carpet was never meant to define you, and it shouldn't. There are more valuable things that make you who you are."

"Like what?"

"Well, you did a very noble thing by wishing for Zinnia's father. You did it to save Taj of course, but I think you did it also for her."

"I did."

Nadar nodded.

Dodie was quiet a minute before asking, "You never told me what you wished for from your last race."

Nadar smiled. "When I raced in my last Grand Flyer and won, Taj was a few years old. Your parents wanted more children, but your mother couldn't conceive again." He looked down at his grandson. "So I wished for you."

Dodie swallowed.

"To my great sadness, that wish came with an unforeseen price, and your mother left us when you were born." Nadar rested a wrinkled hand on top of Dodie's head. "I always told you that you were special."

Dodie did not say anything as a shooting star

streaked overhead.

"So tell me again about the Grand Renegade," he said after a few moments.

Nadar chuckled. "Only racers who've come in first, second, and third in the Grand Flyers can compete. It usually takes place the year following the Grand Flyer. I expect you'll get an invitation within the month."

"Really?" Dodie exclaimed, his heartbeat quickening. "Should I do it?"

"You should consider it."

"Is it more dangerous? Are there different rules? What's the grand prize?"

Nadar chuckled again. "Don't worry, I will tell you all about it some other time. Right now, I want to hear another story. Tell me more about your Grand Flyer."

✦

"**S**o you'll give me proper flying lessons?" Dodie asked as he chased his brother up to the roof.

"You don't need flying lessons," Taj called back as he bounded up the stairs two at a time. "You won the Grand Flyer!"

"But I had help," argued Dodie. "From *Phoenix*, from Grandpapa's map, from Zinnia. My flying isn't that great. I could improve some skills."

"Yeah, you could," said Zinnia as she landed *Amethyst* on their roof patio. With a grin, she hopped off her rug. "Your threading is weak."

"Hey!" Dodie frowned. "You said it wasn't bad!"

Zinnia giggled. "I was being nice. Actually we *both* could use some threading lessons. I haven't figured it out yet either."

"Alright," consented Taj as he mounted *Sand Surfer*. "Lesson one: Threading. Now pay attention or you'll both be kicked out of Taj's Flying Academy."

Dodie rolled his eyes and Zinnia giggled again. They climbed onto their racer rugs and followed Taj down into the alley behind the emporium. Taj gave good instructions and helped them with their form. By the end of the hour, Dodie and Zinnia were able to thread the alley wall. They returned to the roof for a little breather before practicing more. Taj entertained them with some fancy flying maneuvers.

"I got an invitation to race in the Grand Renegade," said Dodie as he plopped down on a straw mat. He absent-mindedly fiddled with the good luck charm strung around his neck.

Zinnia sat down. "Are you gonna do it?"

"I don't know." Dodie watched Taj do an upside-down loop in the air. "It's supposed to be more intense than the Grand Flyer. I only raced the Grand Flyer for Taj. What would I be racing the Renegade for?"

"For yourself," said Zinnia. "I think with some training from Taj you could do it."

Dodie looked at her. "Really?"

Zinnia smiled and her eyes looked fondly at him. "If you do it, you have to promise me something."

Dodie's heartbeat quickened, as usually happened when he was around her. "Anything."

"Promise you'll come back alive," she said, her pretty face looking solemn.

They locked eyes for a moment, and Dodie felt lost in the fire in her eyes.

She cleared her throat and said in a lighter tone, "I don't wanna have to beat a bunch of boys again and win the Grand Flyer to wish you back to me."

Dodie grinned. "Yeah, I like your hair growing out. You shouldn't have to cut it again."

Zinnia blushed slightly as she tucked a strand behind one ear.

Taj skidded to a landing next to them. "Lesson two—"

"Will you coach me for the Grand Renegade?" Dodie interrupted.

Taj gave a lop-sided smile. "If you split the prize with me fifty-fifty."

"Thirty-seventy," Zinnia piped up as she crossed her arms.

Taj chuckled. "What are you, his manager? Forty-sixty."

Dodie stuck out his hand. "Deal."

Taj pulled Dodie into an affectionate headlock. "Let's get started!"

About the Author

F.C. Shaw started writing stories when she was eight years old. She loves children's stories, Sherlock Holmes, and mysteries, so had to write a book combining all three. She spends her afternoons writing for kids, and her nights dreaming of new stories. She lives with her husband and two sons in a home they have ambitiously dubbed The Manor in Santa Maria, California. When she's not plotting stories, she teaches visual arts in local schools and enjoys a good game of Scrabble.

Discover More Remarkable Books
from Future House Publishing

Never miss a book release.
Sign up for the Future House Publishing email list.

www.futurehousepublishing.com

www.facebook.com/FutureHousePublishing

http://twitter.com/FutureHousePub